State of Emergency

Collapse Series #1

Summer Lane

For Mom & Dad.

Thanks for believing that writing is a real job.

Prologue

I don't know how it happened. Nobody does. There are only theories, empty rhetoric and doomsday prophecies. None of them are right, but none of them are completely wrong, either. They all have a grain of truth. All I know is where I was and what I was doing when it happened.

The day had started out like any other. I hit the snooze button on my alarm before dragging myself out of bed. I combed back my long red hair, threw on some clothes, and went into the kitchen. As usual, no one had gone to the grocery store, so breakfast consisted of burnt toast and a teaspoon of olive oil.

Because fatty acids are supposed to be healthy for you.

And because there's nothing else to eat in my house except a can of string beans from the nineties.

Being nineteen, graduated from high school and unemployed, I didn't have much to do besides surf the internet looking for interesting stories and reading my stack of books from the library. Lately I had applied for a multitude of different jobs, including flight attendant, car washer and hotel manager. Needless to say, none of those positions panned out.

I'm more of the independent type, getting paid by my dad to help him out with *his* job as a private detective. He's been letting me poke around in his cases since I was a freshman in high school. I'm good at it, too. Criminal justice. I even wanted a degree in it, but since I'm broke and stuck in a two-bedroom home with an empty refrigerator, my options are slim.

After I looked for a few jobs online, I closed my laptop and began cleaning the house. My dad and I lived in a small home in the outer suburbs of Los Angeles. Culver City, to be exact. It's around ten minutes away from Hollywood. The land of spray-on tans and yoga classes.

It's a nice place to live as long as you stay on the good side of town. If you drive too far in any direction, you'll end up in a ghetto. A visit to the grocery store might end up becoming a drive-by shooting.

Unsurprisingly, I'm an introvert.

So that day, that regular, average day, turned out to be a day that not only changed *my* life, by everyone else's.

It was the day technology turned on us.

It was the beginning of a major pain in the butt.

Chapter One

It's exactly 6:32 p.m. on December 10th. I know, because I'm texting my dad, telling him that I'm going to bring home Chinese takeout for dinner when the screen goes dead.

I'm talking *died*.

The battery gets hot in my hand. The digital clock in my car disappears. I'm idling on the side of a busy curb in Culver City. I pop the battery out of my phone and put it back in. Nothing.

And that's when I notice that the car is silent.

Off. Dead.

I turn the key a few times in the ignition, getting nothing from the engine. It won't even *try* to start. I look out my window. Every streetlight, lamp, apartment window and neon bar sign shuts off simultaneously.

I watch as a boulevard of cars die. Headlights disappear, engines cut out. Vehicles crash and smash against everything in sight. Someone screams.

Probably me.

I crawl out of my car and stand on the sidewalk. Everyone is reaching for their cell phones. It's their first instinct. Their initial reaction. But it's a no-go. Our phones are dead. Non-responsive.

That isn't the worst of it.

I turn. Los Angeles is clearly visible in the distance, its signature circular skyscraper lit up like a Christmas tree. I have a brief feeling of comfort knowing that the electricity is still on over there. Emphasis on *brief*. The tower goes black, as does the rest of the city.

Just like *that* the entire region is plummeted into complete, utter
darkness.

At first, people are relatively calm.

I mean, power outages *do* happen.

But cars dying?

Cell phones melting?

Digital watches flickering out?

What kind of a freak thing is *that*?

I have an idea, but I say nothing. I'm smart enough to know how
quickly a panicked crowd can turn into a mob, so I keep my mouth
shut and remain on the sidewalk. How am I going to get home? A
sea of unmoving cars stretches from here to the city limits – if not
farther. It's been a good twenty minutes since everything died.
Cops or ambulances should have been here in ten minutes.

Are their cars dead, too?

What about traffic helicopters? Those babies are *always* hovering
over LA, doing regular traffic checkups. Instead everything is silent:
A graveyard of cars. The unlit buildings are their headstones.

As confusion rises, people get out of their cars. One lady is crying.
Her vehicle won't start. Her cell phone won't work.

Welcome to the club.

I don't notice anyone injured but...suddenly I hear a distant
humming sound. I strain to tell what it is, wondering if it's the
cavalry finally on its way.

It's about *time*.

But it doesn't get louder, just closer. Like wind whistling through
an empty tunnel. I search the skies for aircraft.

Everyone else is searching, too. Confused. The darkness is deep and permeating, and the lights of a helicopter or an airplane are nowhere to be seen.

That is, until it hits. I feel the ground shake beneath my feet as a hulking mass streaks above our heads, barely visible against the night sky.

I am so shocked – so terrified - that I can't move. I watch in fear as a plane descends like a missile into the heart of the city, colliding with the ground. The impact is unbelievable. The shockwave hits my chest like a wall of bricks. I am thrown backwards, hitting the ground with a *thud*. My eardrums begin to ring. I struggle for breath, kneeling, watching. Awestruck and horrified.

A volley of flames erupts in the distance. It lights up the dark city, a massive bonfire reaching to the heavens. I can feel the heat on my face. People shout. Scream.

The Los Angeles International Airport isn't far away.

If airplanes are falling out of the sky...

I scramble to my feet, my terror palpable, turning my mouth dry. I don't know what's happening but I *do* know this:

I have to get off the streets.

I wrap the strap of my purse around my wrist and stumble forward several steps, my head spinning from the explosion of the plane. I see others doing the same thing; fumbling for balance, clawing their way upright, crying. Panicked.

The buildings are bathed in dull, orange light.

To abstain from dissolving into panic myself, I count to one-hundred over and over as I walk down the streets, moving with purpose. I move as fast as I can, breaking into a sprint as I round the corner. The street here goes underneath the 405, L.A.'s busiest freeway. There are people standing on the edges of the overpass, pointing and yelling, looking at the airplane in the distance.

By now I'm breathing hard. I keep moving under the freeway, running along the sidewalk. A man wearing baggy pants and a backwards baseball cap steps onto the road.

"What's going on, man?" he asks the guy next to him.

"I don't know. I don't understand..." the stranger replies, fear in his eyes. "Is it a terrorist attack?"

I concentrate on walking, avoiding eye contact, only one thing on my mind:

Get home.

Get home and find dad.

Home is almost three miles from here. I can make it if I move quickly. When emergency vehicles get here the streets will be blocked and locked down for hours. I need to squeeze through *now*.

"Oh, my god!" A woman in a beanie exclaims. "It's another one!"

I turn around, watching as another airplane descends dangerously low over the city. The same screeching, ripping sound fills the air. The mass of metal dips low over the skyline.

I break out into a dead run.

A few beats later, it strikes the ground. The impact isn't as intense as the first detonation. It's farther away. It still shakes the ground and sends a shockwave across the city. I stagger, struggling to stay upright. Fighting the pressure of the shockwave.

"Come on..." I mutter, looking at my cell phone again. It's still dead. Nothing is turning it back on. I stuff it back in my pocket, ducking onto a side street off the main boulevard. Residents are coming out of their apartments, restaurants and nail salons. The air is crisp and cold, burning my throat with every breath.

And every block it's the same. Lights are off, cars are frozen on the streets, people are forming crowds, looking to the skies as another plane passes over the city. Streets are becoming gridlocked with frightened people.

Mass confusion and panic has begun.

I avoid them. I steer clear of the busier streets, the large groups of people. I manage to turn over a three-mile walk in less than an hour despite the crowds.

By the time I reach my neighborhood, the city is loud with white noise: the sound of chaos. The sound of fear. Explosions ring through the air. The ground continually shakes with the impact of falling jets and planes.

And the street is dark. No quaint houses glowing with interior lighting tonight.

Tonight the light is gone.

Tonight everything is different.

I reach my house. It's blue with white trim. A garden of dead zinnias border the front steps. I take the keys out of my purse with shaking hands, jam it into the lock and open the front door. I slam it shut behind me.

"Candles, candles," I say aloud, feeling my way into the kitchen. I open the cupboard under the sink and pull out the emergency candles. I light the wicks with matches hidden in the utensil drawer, illuminating the dull yellow paint on the walls. I flick the light switches up and down. I try turning on the TV. I mess with the radio.

Nothing, nothing, nothing.

Okay. What do I do?

The power is out. The cell phones are dead. The cars are busted. The airplanes are falling out of the sky. The situation isn't looking rosy.

I stop and sit on the couch, holding my head in my hands in the dark.

Breathe in, breathe out. Don't panic.

I think about the many conversations I've had with my father about emergency protocol. As a cop, he's seen plenty of people in high-stress situations. It always pays to be ready, he told me. Most people are unprepared for an emergency. They get scared and start raiding grocery stores for food and water when a crisis hits. They'll break into houses. Vandalize apartments. Steal supplies.

One minute? Civilized. The next? Psycho rioters.

I get up.

One step at a time, I think.

I take a candle to my bedroom and open the closet. There is a go-bag inside, compliments of my father's insistence that I have an emergency plan in the event of a nuclear attack. Or in this case, a massive power outage and malfunctioning technology.

I grab the backpack and unzip the largest compartment, walking hurriedly from one end of the house to the other. I cram an old photo album inside. A small, spare blanket. An extra box of matches.

I drag the bag into the living room and throw open the hall closet.

Boom.

A powerful impact shakes the house. I grab the wall to keep from falling over. A blast of orange light ignites about three miles away from my house. I can clearly see it through the front window.

Another airplane. They're falling faster.

I can't stay here. I can't wait for dad. He could be anywhere.

I have to get out.

Calm, calm, calm, I repeat. *I got this.*

I pull a smaller bag from the closet and throw it on the couch, unzipping it with trembling fingers. There are two weapons inside. A semi-automatic handgun and my grandfather's antique pistol. I take the semi-auto and strap the holster around my waist, hiding it under my jacket. I know my father is already armed wherever he is, so I put Grandpa's pistol in my backpack and dump the boxes of ammo into the side pocket. It's heavy.

Don't panic, don't panic.

That's my mantra.

I zip everything up, toss in some candles and lace up my combat boots. I bought them this year because I thought they'd look trendy. Now I'm glad I have them. They're going to be practical.

The radio!

I suddenly remember our emergency radio. I slide into the kitchen and open one of the shallow drawers. In the back, there is a small, metallic box. I pop it open and take a radio out. A satisfied smile crosses my face. The box is made out of ferrite, a type of metal resistant to technological attacks, or as my dad would say, "e-bombs."

I wind up the manual crank radio and turn it on. There is no sound, only static. And then I turn it to another station, and another, and another.

Because every station is saying the same thing.

"If you can hear this, this is not a drill. Stay inside and seek shelter. If you are not in your home, find shelter immediately…"

My blood runs ice cold. I shut the radio off and shove it into my coat pocket.

The only piece of technology in the house that's working is the radio: the one thing that was protected in the ferrite case.

I pray to God that doesn't mean what I think it does.

I grab the backpack, take one last look at the house and head toward the back door. Once outside, I pause and listen. Usually you would hear sirens or helicopters or bullhorns telling people to shut up and let the emergency workers do their job.

Instead I'm hearing the sound of a warzone.

Shuddering, I head toward the alley, where my dad and I built a small garage. I open it and step inside, using the flashlight to navigate through the piles of tools and machinery.

And I look at my escape vehicle.

It's a 78 Mustang Dad and I worked on together. While I'm not an automobile expert by any stretch, I *do* know that it should run as long as I have gasoline in the tank. We installed ferrite cores, a protective cage made out of the same metal that was keeping the radio safe in the kitchen drawer. Its main purpose is to guard a piece of technology from an electromagnetic pulse – which is what I think just wiped out every piece of microchip-based technology in Los Angeles.

Because that's what an EMP does. It kills computers. My Mustang doesn't use a computer chip to start up, unlike most of the cars on the road. It should be unaffected. I throw my backpack in the passenger seat and check the trunk. There are a few sealed cans of gasoline, a box of tools with replacement parts for the vehicle and three cases of bottled water.

Always be prepared, Dad used to say. Why do parents always have to know everything? I slam the trunk shut and get in the driver's seat.

"Please start," I pray. "Please, please, please…"

I turn the key in the ignition.

Please.

It turns over. The engine rumbles to life. The smell of gasoline fills the room. I open the garage door and back up, coasting into the alley. I keep my headlights off. I don't need to draw attention to the fact that I'm one of the only people in the city with a working car.

That could be seriously dangerous.

I hit the road and step on it, doing sixty on the boulevard. As I get closer to the more populated areas I have to avoid frozen cars. Civilians perk up as I approach, pointing and yelling when my car roars by. It makes me nervous. *Way* nervous.

I've seen *War of the Worlds*.

"Okay, Dad," I say, gripping the steering wheel. "I know where to find you. You'd better know where to find me."

Chapter Two

I had a pretty normal family.

My mother was the manager of a chain hotel in Culver City. I didn't see her very often. My father was a Los Angeles cop. He worked at night and slept during the day, which meant that the curtains in our house were always closed.

My mother's dream for my life was to send me to a topnotch boarding school in Europe. Of course, my parents couldn't afford an education like that, so the idea was eventually canned.

Dad was different. He actually seemed to *like* having me around. He enrolled me in a charter school program. I only had to go to a class three times a week. The rest of my homework was completed at home.

I loved the charter school. I was a shy kid. Terrified of my own shadow, Dad used to say. I spent most of my time at home, catching glimpses of my parents when they were visiting between shifts. I didn't make friends easily, so I had few.

I preferred the company of silence.

When I was eight years old, my parents divorced. It didn't affect me in the way you'd think it would. I was already used to seeing my parents living apart, so the shock of the separation came as no surprise to me. Dad won the custody battle and mom scored basic visitation rights.

I only visited Mom a few times a year, despite the fact that she lived nearby. I think it was because I was angry with her. For years, it seemed to me that her only goal in life was to send me to a school abroad. I felt unwanted. Unneeded. So I figured, *Why hang around with someone who doesn't want to be with me?*

My father, Frank Hart, was in the military as a young man. He entered the police academy when he was twenty-five. He was on the Los Angeles police force for thirty years before he retired and became a private detective.

I was rarely able to spend time with him, but the difference between his love and my mother's love for me was worlds apart. Mom wanted to dump my butt in a boarding school. Dad wanted me to live at home.

My father was also one of *those* people that believed a national emergency could happen at any moment. He'd dealt with the Los Angeles riots during the 90s and seen all kinds of crazy crap as a cop. Murders, abuse, suicides. He was the kind of person that hoped for the best but expected the worst. His belief that bad things could happen on a dime turned into a hobby. I thought it was a cool pastime. Entertaining. It was one of the few things we were able to do *together.*

Dad's hobby of prepping is why we have emergency go-bags in every room of the house and a pre-planned rendezvous point. It's all suddenly becoming an outstanding idea, given the fact that my father's paranoid prophecy about Los Angeles becoming the immediate site of Armageddon is coming true.

This is a nightmare. I will wake up. I **have** *to wake up.*

I am racing down a little-known back road in Los Angeles, curving around the city and away from the freeway.

"If there's ever a crisis in Los Angeles, like a natural disaster or a terrorist attack," Dad told me, "we need to count on the fact that the

Internet and cell towers will go down. There won't be any electricity, so if we get separated we have to know where to rendezvous."

In retrospect, my dad is a genius. The two of us own a little cabin in the Sierra Nevada Mountains, not too far away from Kings Canyon National Park. It's beautiful, secluded and supplied with emergency goodies. Our plan was that if we ever got separated for some reason, we would meet at the cabin. And now, with the entire city swarming like ants escaping a flooded anthill, it was the wisest decision we ever made.

As I drive I keep my headlights on only when I am far enough away from heavily populated areas. This road is windy. Definitely the *long* way out of the city, but I don't want to risk getting stuck in a panicked mob.

"Give me *something*," I say out loud, turning the portable radio up to full volume. Only bits and pieces of an emergency broadcast come through. I catch snippets like, "electromagnetic pulse," "seek shelter," and "terrorist attack." Those words send a chill up my spine. *Who* and *what* is behind such a devastating attack on Los Angeles? And were *we* the only ones who were hit?

I take a few calming breaths. An anxiety attack behind the wheel of a moving vehicle would be detrimental to my health, so I concentrate on navigating the winding, empty road. I continue to look out my windows, craning my head toward the sky, keeping an eye out for airplanes. If an EMP *did* hit, any aircraft in the sky would plummet to earth immediately. I'm safe for now. I think.

I scream.

Someone is standing in the middle of the two-lane highway. A man. He's perfectly still, looking directly into my headlights. No fear. No hesitation. Pure idiocy.

I slam on the brakes. My car screeches. The smell of burning rubber is harsh and pungent. I twist the steering wheel in an attempt to swerve out of the lane, barely missing him by a foot or two. My car skids, drifts, and turns in a full circle. I take my foot off the brakes as I'm thrown forward against the wheel. No airbag. The car screams to a halt, puffs of smoke filling the air.

Panting for breath, I try to get my senses together. I focus my vision on the road. The man is moving toward my car. Quickly. I throw the car in reverse, hitting the gas. Yet something makes me slow down. Something makes me hesitate. Curiosity? No. Stupidity? Okay, maybe a little.

But it's not that. It's something else.

The man waves his hands back and forth.

"Wait!" he says. "I'm a soldier!"

At the word *soldier* I pause for a moment. He's wearing jeans, but no uniform. Just a green tee shirt. I can't see his face, but his hair is long and drawn back in a ponytail. There's no way he's active duty military.

And then I see the blood.

His shirt is stained with it. I inhale quickly, alarmed, and open the door. Pure instinct. I know that I shouldn't be doing this, but my body moves faster than my brain. This man is hurt. I can't ignore that. I have to do *something*.

Be careful, Cassidy, a little voice warns. *He could be dangerous.*

"What happened?" I ask, stepping outside, keeping the engine running. It's freezing. 11:30 p.m. We're alone on the back roads of the lesser-known Hollywood hills. "Oh, God...how bad are you hurt? What happened?"

Wary, I keep my distance, sliding my hand underneath my coat for the semi-automatic. I have no desire to use it – and don't ever plan on it – but it gives me some confidence to know that I have *something* to defend myself with.

"Easy," he says, lifting up his hands. "I'm not going to hurt you."

"Prove it."

He wiggles his fingers. They're bloody.

"I just need a ride," he says. "If you're headed north."

"I didn't stop to give you a ride," I reply, opening the door to the backseat. "I stopped to see if I could help you with all that blood."

I quickly search through my backpack and pull out a first-aid kit. He watches me, motionless, standing in the glare and shadows of the headlights.

"You got a name or what?" I ask.

"You tell me yours and I'll tell you mine."

I smirk and wave him over, keeping my weapon accessible. "What happened to you?" I say.

He walks closer. His body is tense, but from pain or stress I can't tell. Closer to me I note how tall he is. He's also *very* muscular. Not that I care, but facts are facts. His face is handsome, lined with a thin beard that would accentuate his long hair nicely if it weren't smudged with sweat and grease.

"Long story," he grunts. "I can do this."

"It's *my* stuff. I'll do it," I snap. "Where?"

He pulls the sleeve of his shirt up, revealing a strong arm with a deep cut. It's crusted with dried blood. There also seems to be pieces of glass stuck in the skin.

"What's in your skin?" I ask, swallowing.

"Glass."

"How...?"

"Accident. Five miles back. When everything went out."

"You might have a concussion." I stand on my tiptoes to flush the wound with a bottle of water. It's not bleeding too badly – nothing that will kill him, anyway. A rush of heat bolts up my arm when our hands accidentally touch. I draw back instantly, embarrassed. He doesn't seem to notice.

"Have you seen the city?" I ask.

"Part of it." A muscle ticks in his jaw. "You?"

"I was there." My hands begin to shake. "There were *airplanes* falling out of the sky. Everything died at the same time. Crowds were everywhere..." I trail off. "They're telling people to find shelter if they're not at home."

"Without cars people won't be going anywhere." His eyes dart toward my Mustang.

I bite my lip and say, "I know."

I take a pair of tweezers and use them to pull the most obvious shards of glass out of his skin. It's one of the grossest things I've ever done. And the fact that my hands are trembling doesn't help matters any.

The man gently takes my wrist and holds it, shifting his position. Our eyes lock. He turns his gaze downward, giving me the once-over from head to toe. I blush, flustered.

15

But I don't move.

"How old are you?" he asks. "Where's your family?"

"I'm old enough," I reply, slipping out of his grasp. "Let me wrap that for you."

I take out my medical tape, dry the wound and wrap it with a bandage. He stands there, silent.

"You're alone," he states gravely.

"What's it to you?" My hand inches toward my gun.

Noticing my anxiety, he makes an effort to relax his stance.

"I'm just trying to help," he says. "I'm a Navy SEAL. I'm not a bad guy."

"Sounds like something a bad guy would say," I snort.

"I'm going to be straight with you. I need a ride."

"My dad told me never to talk to strangers, much less give them rides." I shut the back door. "I shouldn't have even stopped."

"But you did." The corners of his mouth curve upward. "Thank you."

I pause, sitting down on the driver's seat. One leg in, one leg out. "You're welcome," I say. I place my hand on the door. "And you're not an active duty Navy SEAL. Your hair is *way* too long."

"I'm a *former* SEAL," he shrugs.

"So you lied," I mutter.

"No. I *am* a soldier. And I can pay you for a ride, if that's what you want," he says.

"I don't want money."

"Look," he says. "I just need to get to Squaw Valley. It's right below Sequoia National Park."

I close my eyes.

Of course.

Squaw Valley is in the foothills, about forty miles below our emergency cabin.

"What's your name?" I ask again.

"Chris," he says. "Chris Young."

I exhale dramatically, blowing my bangs out of my eyes.

"I can take you," I reply.

"But if you try *anything*, I'll shoot you right between the eyes. Seriously."

He almost smiles.

"Yes, ma'am."

I nod. "Get in. I'm wasting gas."

"Let me get my gear." He walks to the side of the road and grabs a backpack and jacket, coming around to the passenger side. It's a military-issue backpack. His jacket is leather.

"Are you a biker?" I ask.

"*Was*," he says.

"The pulse got your bike?"

"Totaled it."

"You're lucky you're alive, you know that?"

He flashes a brilliant smile.

"I know."

*Now **that** is a smile.*

I press down on the accelerator, eager to get the heck out of here. Chris's presence in my car puts me on edge. How many times over the course of my young life has my father warned me never to talk to strangers and *never* get in a car with one?

A lot.

Well, guess what? The world's turned into a freaking Armageddon and I'm going to do what I want. Besides, Chris might come in handy. He's a military guy. Tough, by the looks of it. This could be a positive thing.

"So what's *your* name?" he asks, relaxed against the seat. His voice is deep. Just the hint of a southern accent. "Are you going to tell me?"

"Cassidy," I say. "But you can call me Cassie."

"All right, Cassie," he replies, serious. "What's a kid like you doing with a vintage piece of work like this?"

"You mean my car?"

"No, I mean your shoes."

"Shut up." I find myself smiling. "It's my dad's. I mean, it's *both* of ours."

Silence.

I turn up the radio, discouraged when nothing but static comes through yet again. "Where are you from?" I ask at last.

"San Diego."

"What were you doing in Los Angeles?"

"Weekend bike ride." He looks sideways at me. "And you?"

"I live in Culver City," I shrug.

"Where are your parents?"

"Seriously? Do I really look *that* young?" I press down on the accelerator a little more, giving into my unconscious habit of flooring it when I'm irritated.

"Yeah," Chris says. "You do."

I press my lips together. How much should I tell him?

I finally say, "I got separated from my dad. I'm going to meet him somewhere."

"How far are you driving?"

"Toward Squaw Valley," I reply, vague.

"You're going to keep it a secret?" He smiles. "You're what...sixteen?"

"I'm *nineteen*. Come on. At least *try* to guess accurately."

"Sorry," he says, holding his hands up. "I'm just trying to figure you out."

"You're doing a lousy job." I keep my eyes trained on the road, taking the curves slow and the straightaways like a racecar driver on steroids. "I don't trust you yet, by the way. Keep that in mind."

"Duly noted." His voice is heavy with amusement. "I'll try not to tick you off."

I shake my head.

"Good luck with *that*."

"Look." Chris points to a spot of light ahead on the road. "Turn off the headlights."

I switch the headlights off and we peer into the darkness. There appears to be a group of people on the road, nearly invisible at night.

"They're blocking the road," Chris says. "Turn the car around."

"I can't! I'm doing sixty!"

"Then slow down and make a U-turn."

His words are casual, yet commanding. I do as he says. It's almost instinctual to take his advice. I lift my foot off the gas but we're still moving too quickly toward the group. I stomp on the brake. We're thrown forward as the car comes to a sudden halt. Chris peers out the window. Some of the group breaks away from the rest of the crowd and begins moving toward us. Fast.

"Keep the doors locked," he says calmly. "Just drive."

The people, who are mostly bathed in shadow, are yelling angrily. And they're running. They bang their fists against the windows. I can't make out a single discernible statement, but the overall message appears to be:

"We're taking your car and we're not giving it back."

Just a guess.

"Okay, punch it!" Chris commands. "*Right now.*"

"I am!" I yell, coiled tight. I hit the accelerator and flip a U-turn. Something hits the right rear window. I scream. Someone from the mob has grabbed the door handle. He holds on as we gain speed. His shoes scrape against the pavement.

"Don't stop," Chris warns. "That's what he wants you to do."

I look over my left shoulder and see a flash of a young man wearing a skullcap. His eyes are wild, desperate. And then he lets go. I hear his body smack against the road. Bile rises in the back of my throat. What have I done? Have I killed him?

How can I leave him dead on the road?

"Don't do it," Chris says, moving closer. "That's a mob. A *dangerous* one. People are going to act like this for a long time until the power comes back on. They'll take what you have if they can and leave you to die."

Isn't that what I just did? Did I just leave someone to die?

I grip the steering wheel until my knuckles turn white. Tears fill my eyes. Stupid, stupid tears.

"Why?" I whisper.

Chris studies my profile in the dark cab. Thinking.

"Because civilization as we know it is gone," he says at last.

Chapter Three

I don't know if I've mentioned this, but I'm a realist. Most people would say that's the same thing as being a pessimist, but it's not. Really. I just look at something and don't expect anything great to come of it. I'm simply that way. If you hope for something good, you're going to be disappointed. I side with reality and most of the time we get along just fine.

So naturally, the end of the world as we know it doesn't come as a complete shock to me, although it puts a serious question mark on whether or not I'll be able to go bowling next Tuesday.

"So who do you think is behind this?" I ask Chris.

It's around four in the morning. We've tried five different roads that lead out of Los Angeles. All of them have been blocked with mobs waiting to hijack operating vehicles. The route we're currently driving is a last ditch effort to escape Los Angeles without leaving the car behind.

"I heard something about the Chinese on the radio before we lost the signal," I continue, yawning. "I bet they did it."

"I don't know." Chris props his boots up on the dashboard. "It's hard to say."

"Why? Is there a secret love fest between China and America I don't know about?"

"I was in the military for nine years," he replies. "I've seen a lot of different enemies of the United States around the world. I don't think China is behind this."

"Then who is?" I say, exasperated. "What if it's not an attack? What if it's just an accident?"

"You seriously think an electromagnetic pulse is an accident?" Chris chuckles. "Yeah, it could have been caused by a solar flare, but I doubt it."

"You don't know any more than I do," I say. "You're just spit balling."

"Who isn't?" He looks out the window, staring at the sky. "This could be more widespread than we think. What if L.A. wasn't the only city hit with this thing?"

I shiver.

"Then there's no place to escape to."

Chris turns back toward me. "This is the last route out of here. If it's blocked..." He lets the sentence hang in the air between us. Civilians are acting like maniacal psychopaths. Mobs are everywhere. It's not safe to go back *into* the city.

"Then what?" I ask, voicing our twin concerns.

"Then we find another way."

I yawn again, exhausted. This road is a two-lane highway. It's old. It winds throughout the smaller hills above Hollywood, dodging the freeways and dipping close to residential areas. Off in the distance there are sparks of orange light. Fires.

"I haven't seen any planes for a while," I mutter.

"Most modern passenger planes have faraday cages," Chris replies. "They're protected from EMPs."

"Then what about the ones that fell out of the sky in Culver City?" I ask. "Those things were like bombs."

"They obviously weren't protected well enough." Chris stretches. "I can drive. You look like you're going to fall asleep."

"I probably am."

"I'll take over."

"Sorry. Nobody drives the Mustang but me."

Chris shakes his head. After another forty-five minutes we reach the other side of the hills, signaling the break out of Hollywood. I roll to a stop at the top of a rise, looking down over the beginning of the small mountain range.

Total darkness.

I just stare at it.

Who knows what's out there? The freeway will be filled with dead cars. Evacuees will be attempting to find transportation. Some of them will be fleeing on foot.

"Cassie?" Chris says.

I snap out of it.

"Yeah?" I reply, shaky. "I'm fine."

But I'm *so* not. The world is coming to an end.

Who could be fine with that?

When late morning hits, I fall asleep at the wheel. We've spent the last three hours navigating old roads in the middle of nowhere in order to avoid jammed freeways and populated areas. It was a difficult thing to do, since the maps I have in the car aren't specific when it comes to the back roads. By the time the sun is warm enough to make me sleepy, I can't take it anymore.

My head lolls forward and hits the steering wheel. The car swerves to the left. I jerk awake, realizing with horrified clarity what I've done. But Chris is there. His hands are on the steering wheel, his long legs moving my feet out of the way. I jerk backwards and Chris slams on the brakes, pulling the car to the side of the road.

Chris seems to realize that he's nearly sitting on top of me and draws back. Quickly. "Let me drive," is all he says. No chastisement. No lecture on how falling asleep at the wheel was *my* fault for pushing myself too far.

As for me, my heart is beating out of my chest. I simply nod, mumbling something about having to use the restroom, and open the driver door. The air is crisp and cutting. Chris walks around the back of the car and, for the first time, I see my new traveling companion in daylight.

His hair is golden brown. A thin scar trails from the inside of his wrist to his elbow. His eyes are green. *Electric* green. I find myself frozen, staring like an idiot. He's incredible.

Breathtaking, even.

I inhale slowly, blinking.

And the corner of his mouth begins to curve upwards. My hands automatically fly to my face. Oh, my God. I'm *blushing*.

Being pale does little to hide emotions.

"It's all yours," I say, avoiding eye contact. "But if you crash or scratch her, I'll shoot you."

Placing his hand on the door above my head, he replies, "I'll remember that."

For one intense moment we lock gazes. A weight drops on my chest. I'm unable to breathe, unable to move. Trapped between the car door and his body.

I exhale and step away.

"I have to pee," I say quickly.

In retrospect I realize that probably wasn't the most seductive thing to say after a hot staring contest. But hey. The truth is the truth.

Chris smirks.

"Be my guest. I won't steal the car."

"Don't even think about it," I warn, grinning. I pat my gun for effect, grab the car keys and walk off the asphalt.

When I'm done I walk back to the car, half expecting it to be gone. But Chris is still standing there, waiting patiently. I give him a funny look. Surprised, I guess, that he didn't hotwire the car and supplies, I throw open the passenger door.

"I'm impressed," I state.

Chris slides behind the wheel.

"I knew you would be," he replies.

A few strands of hair have escaped from his ponytail, accentuating the angles of his face. I'm tempted to reach out and brush them into place, but I don't. We're not *that* chummy.

"So what's in Squaw Valley for you?" I ask, closing my eyes.

He doesn't answer right away. I curl up and lean my head against the window. "Family," he replies.

"Don't tell me. They're doomsday preppers," I quip.

"Something like that." Chris raises an eyebrow. "You're quite a prepper yourself."

"Thanks to my dad," I say. My eyes sting with unshed tears. "He always believed we should be prepared for an emergency."

"Your father is a very wise man," Chris nods. "Was he in the military?"

"For six years," I reply. "Then he was a cop for thirty. Now he's a private detective."

"Impressive," he says.

I close my eyes.

"Maybe." I sigh. "Wake me up if you see anything alarming."

"Like...?"

"Like an airplane dropping on our heads or a band of marauders on the side of the road." I shrug. "Little things like that."

"I'll do that."

"Good."

I go to sleep. I nod off for about two hours. Fortunately, I'm so tired that I don't have any nightmares – ironic, because I can't help from waking up to one. One in which Los Angeles is without power and passenger airplanes are doubling as bombs.

A couple of hours later Chris suddenly shoves me on the shoulder. I slap his hand away, irritated.

"What?" I slur. "Did I miss something?"

"You'll want to see this," he says, his voice flat.

I rub the crud out of my eyes and sit up. After a few blinks to clear my vision, I notice how slow Chris is driving. He's watching something on the road ahead of us. We're driving on the *old* highway that was all but abandoned after the massive Interstate was built into the Tehachapi Mountains – also known as the Grapevine. It's like driving through the countryside, beautiful trees and tall grass swaying all around us.

An object sits on the side of the road.

"Oh, my God!" I gasp. "It's a baby carrier!"

It's tilted sideways on the lip of the old road. There is also a diaper bag and an open suitcase. An older-model car is sitting near all of it, its windows smashed out.

"We have to see if there's a baby inside," I say.

"It's a trap."

"But what if it's not?"

"Cassie..."

I open the door and step outside. Chris yells at me to stay put, swearing like a sailor. Appropriate, I guess, for a Navy SEAL. I jog down the side of the road. Chris opens his door and runs after me, telling me in explicit terms to get back in the car.

Apparently he didn't expect me to exit the vehicle.

"Cassidy, listen to me!" he says. "You don't need to get this close. I didn't want..." his voice falls away as I run up to the baby carrier and kneel down, pulling back the blanket. It's empty. I breathe a sigh of relief. "Thank God," I say.

"Get back in the car," Chris growls. "Now."

"Relax." I stand up, dusting off my jeans. "You're a little high-strung, you know that?"

Chris scowls.

"Don't piss me off, kid."

I glare at him.

"Don't talk to me like that."

Chris steps forward and grabs my arm, half-walking, half-dragging me back to the Mustang. "Let *go* of me!" I say. "Hey, that hurts."

"Be glad you weren't in that car."

I look back at the wrecked vehicle.

"What's that supposed to mean?"

"What do you think they stopped for, Cassie?" he points at the baby carrier. My eyes travel to the ravaged car. I see the tip of a limp, white hand lolling out of the backseat. Droplets of blood are splattered across the broken glass on the ground. I gasp, hands darting to my mouth to avoid gagging.

"Oh, my God... what happened?"

"It's called carjacking," Chris says, walking me back to the car, physically turning me away from the horrible sight. "They prey on the sympathy of people like you, hoping you'll get out of your car to help a baby."

I choke on an ill-concealed sob, more from the horror of the last fifteen hours than anything else.

"How can everything change so fast?" I ask, a tear slipping down my cheek. Chris opens the passenger door and catches the tear with his thumb, green eyes sad but serious.

"Nothing's changed," he says softly. "This crisis will just bring out the worst in people."

He gestures for me to sit. I don't argue. Chris gets back in and pretty soon we're picking up speed again.

"Why didn't they take the parent's car?" I whisper. "Why did they lure them there if they were just going to kill them?"

Chris sighs.

"Their car was an older model, like this Mustang," he replies, his voice hard. "It was probably unaffected by the EMP and whoever was waiting on the side of the road was hoping they'd be able to steal the car. I'm guessing there wasn't enough gas left, so they killed the passengers."

"That's horrible."

"Why do you act so shocked?" he says. "Your dad was a cop for thirty years, right? Stuff like this is common in his world. Especially in LA."

"This is different," I answer, making a Herculean effort not to cry. "This is...*psycho.*"

Chris doesn't answer. Does he agree with me? I don't know. His body is taut with tension, like a coil wound tight, waiting to spring. Perhaps he's not as calm and controlled as he would like me to think.

"Do you have any siblings?" I ask, trying to turn the conversation to something remotely normal.

"Yes." He presses his lips together. "I have a brother."

"Oh. What about your parents?"

He rubs his chin.

"You ask a lot of questions, *you know that?*"

"Yeah, so what? How else am I supposed to get to know you?"

Chris shakes his head, amusement tugging at the corners of his mouth. "We'll need to refill the gas tank again in a minute," he says, changing the subject. "How much do you have left in the trunk?"

"Enough to get us to Squaw Valley," I reply. "But not to our cabin. And that's only if we can avoid any more detours."

"That could be a problem."

"We can stop in a smaller city. Maybe the pulse only hit LA."

"We can't be sure."

"Yeah, but if we run out of gas things will *really* suck." I shrug. "I'd rather take my chances in the city."

Chris mulls the idea over.

"Where's the nearest city?" he asks.

I pull a map out of the passenger door pocket. After studying it I say, "There's a place in Santa Clarita."

"That's right off the freeway," Chris says. "We could get stuck in a gridlock. It might be safer to just siphon off some gas from abandoned cars."

"I agree," I answer. "But we still need to see if Santa Clarita was affected by the EMP. If this thing was limited to Los Angeles, then we have a chance at survival. Besides, Santa Clarita is fairly remote. It might be worth a shot."

Chris nods, wordlessly agreeing.

We need to know how far the EMP stretches.

The more time that elapses since the pulse hit, the more gas will continue to disappear from stations. The more people will panic and start raiding grocery stores for food and water, and the more anarchic society will become.

If this is indeed a widespread thing.

We'll just have to find out how many cities were affected by the pulse, I guess.

Chapter Four

I've seen ghost towns that look friendlier than this. It's hard for me to believe that only fifteen hours ago Los Angeles and every freeway running in and out of the city was moving with high-speed traffic.

Santa Clarita, a long stretch of travel centers and restaurants on the other side of Six Flags Rollercoaster Park, is deserted. There are cars scattered across the interstate, many of them overturned or smashed together in piles. It looks like a junkyard. There are no people in sight. No ambulances, helicopters or police cars.

Just an abandoned McDonald's and a gas station.

Chris eases the Mustang along the road, keeping the window rolled down, listening. His face is pensive, his eyebrows drawn together.

"This is *not* normal," I say, stating the obvious.

He doesn't reply. We continue to coast down the street, dodging a car that crashed into a post. Dark, thick skid marks are smeared across the road. Some of them reach the sidewalk.

"At least we know that Santa Clarita was hit with the pulse, too," I say. "We're at least thirty-five miles out of L.A."

Chris's frown deepens.

"We'll try the gas station," he says. "But don't count on finding any fuel."

"I'm not."

Chris pulls up to the pumps and cuts the engine. We get out. The sky is darkening around the edges with rainclouds. Gusts of cold air blow through the abandoned rest area.

"These pumps are all dead," I say, disappointed.

I had been expecting this. But I wasn't hoping for it.

"They might have some gas cans inside," Chris says, tapping the blank pump screen. "If not, we'll siphon gas from some of these cars. Keep your eyes open."

He reaches into the backseat and pulls out his backpack. He removes a semiautomatic that's a lot newer – and cooler looking – than mine and tucks it into his belt.

"Why are you bringing that? Do you think there's going to be somebody in there to shoot?" I ask, alarmed. "And I didn't know you had a *gun*."

"I didn't want to scare you," he says simply. "Stay here."

"I'm not moving. Geez."

Chris cocks an eyebrow and walks toward the building. I pull my jacket tighter and lean against the pump, overlooking the spooky scene before me. It's as if the populace *disappeared* all at once. But where did they go? How did they get out so quickly?

I grab my crank radio from the front seat. After some windups I shake my arm out and turn up the volume. Crackling static. And then, a short burst of dialogue:

"Citizens should take care to remain where they are and stay inside," it says. A man's voice. Pre-recorded. *"For those that are unable to reach shelter, there are emergency camps in California for refugees. The following is a list of camp locations: Santee, San Bernardino, Bakersfield, Stockton, Elk Grove, Dublin, Yreka, San Jose and Fresno. Again, do not leave your homes unless necessary. Seek shelter at a relief camp or indoors. This is not a drill. The President has declared a State of Emergency. Help is coming."*

33

The audio loops and starts over. I turn from station to station. Every broadcasting center that is still on the air is spouting the same thing. My hand hovers over the off button as I hear those three words again:

State of Emergency.

Apparently the whole state has gone dark.

What about the rest of the country?

God. I hope not.

"Chris!" I call. "You need to hear this!"

No answer. I roll my eyes and toss the radio back in the car. Down the street, the road dips right underneath the freeway overpass. It's completely stacked with cars. A virtual parking lot.

I'd hate to be the cleanup crew who has to take care of *that.*

I walk around the Mustang and check for dents. There's a scratch on the rear fender. I bend to inspect it, my reflection peeking out at me in the shiny chrome.

This is what I get for letting him drive.

And then I see a flicker of movement in the chrome. At first I think it's nothing more than my hair blowing around my face, or Chris returning from the building.

That's before I realize it's another person.

I stand up. On the other end of the McDonald's parking lot, a guy dressed in gangster garb is standing there with his hat on backwards. He's wearing all black, some sort of metal bar in his hand. A crowbar?

Not exactly a positive sign.

He's staring straight at me. Both of us, motionless in the middle of this deserted rest stop. My heart drops to my stomach, not because I'm afraid of *people*, but because I'm afraid that a guy dressed like a gangster holding a crowbar in the middle of Armageddon doesn't have sparkling intentions.

As I expected, he moves toward me. I immediately reach for my gun, keeping my hand on the holster.

"Chris..." I say. "Get *out* here."

No answer.

As gangster boy gets closer, I take note of the myriad of tattoos winding up his arms. Some of them crawl across his cheeks.

"What do you want?" I demand.

He takes a step onto the gas station driveway. The metal object he's carrying *is* a crowbar, and there seems to be something on his leg. Blood? I swallow, fear sending a shiver through my body.

"You all alone?" he asks.

"None of your business," I reply. "What do you want?"

"This *was* a rest stop."

"Was. Now what do you want?"

"I want a ride."

"No can do. I don't give rides to strangers."

Unless their name is Chris Young.

"I didn't ask you if you were going to *give* me one," he says, flashing a dangerous expression. "I said I wanted a ride."

The reality of his words sinks in.

"Get out of here," I order, removing my gun from its holster. My hands are shaking slightly. "Or I'll shoot you..." I pause. "Right between the eyes."

He raises his hands.

"Easy," he says, backing up. "I was just asking. I'm going, I'm going..."

"Good. Go a little faster. Your tattoos are making me dizzy."

Feeling triumphant, I allow myself a smug smile.

It doesn't last.

Someone grabs my arms from behind and twists the gun out of my grip. It happens fast. I have no time to stop it. One minute I'm standing with a stupid smile on my face. The next, my cheek is slammed against the pavement and my hands are shoved into the small of my back.

A boot comes down on my shoulders, pressing me flat.

"Get...off..." I grunt weakly.

My adrenaline spikes. My heart rate skyrockets.

I'm trapped, I'm trapped...I need to move. Think!

"Nice and easy, little girl," he says, leaning down to peek at my face. "You keep quiet and I might and let you live."

I bite back a stinging retort.

"Keep her there, Raymond," Gangster boy says to the guy keeping me down. I can't see his face but he's got the same tattoos on his hands that his friend does.

"Yeah, there's gas in the trunk!" Gangster boy hoots. "She's got food and water, too. Damn. She's even got a radio." He kicks my foot. "What'd you do? Raid a grocery store?"

"I like to stay prepared," I spit, "so I don't have to steal other people's stuff."

Gangster boy laughs.

"Let's get out of here."

The weight on my back vanishes. Gangster boy lifts me up by the collar of my jacket. I cough, struggling for air.

"You're kind of pretty for a little thing," he sneers. He reeks of cigarettes and stale sweat. "Maybe I *will* take you along."

"I'd rather chew glass," I choke out.

Sarcasm has always been my weapon of choice. Unfortunately, it doesn't have any physical power. Gangster boy's friend, Raymond, comes into view. A pale guy with similar gangster garb. He appears unmoved by my predicament.

"We'll see," gangster boy says, twirling his crowbar in one hand. "What do you think?"

Seeing the crowbar prompts me to take action. I bring my combat boot up and kick him as hard as I can in the groin. While he doesn't let go of my jacket, he *does* loosen his grip. I claw my fingernails across his face, sink my teeth into his hand and twist away from his body.

He spits out a string of profanities and drops me. I scramble to my feet and sprint away, heading for the front seat. Raymond is right behind me. He's fast.

I dive for the driver's seat and grab the keys to the Mustang. Raymond drags me out by the belt loop of my jeans. I literally shove the keys into my shirt, hoping they stay hidden in my camisole. Gangster boy grabs me by the neck, cursing and spitting. He slams my body against the cement pillar that supports the awning over the gas station. I gasp, feeling the air rush out of my lungs. He grabs me again and tosses me to the ground, kicking me in the stomach. I double over in pain, covering the back of my neck with my hands. Bursts of color ignite before my eyes.

Idiot, I think. *How do I get out of this?*

He swings his crowbar through the air. I roll out of the way, narrowly avoiding a blow to the head. I spring to my feet, ducking behind the pillar. His crowbar hits the concrete, ringing loudly with another failed attempt to bring me down. I slide around the pillar. Raymond is there. He slams into me, sending me sprawling. Gangster boy is behind me. Both of them are closing in. He swipes his crowbar through the air. It collides with my lower hip. A bolt of fiery pain consumes me.

"Stop!" I scream. I crumple to the ground, grasping my hip, gritting my teeth. "Please, don't!"

Gangster boy slams the crowbar toward me again. There is no mercy in his eyes. I cover my face with my arm, instinctively protecting my head.

Bam!

I feel no further pain.

I peek through my hands, shocked. Chris's powerful arm is blocking the crowbar. He stands protectively in front of me. He whips his hand underneath the bar, twists it out of Gangster boy's hand and slams it against his head.

No hesitation. All business.

Gangster boy goes down, collapsing like a rag doll. Raymond pauses, assessing his new enemy, and advances on Chris.

I take a step backwards. Chris twirls the crowbar in his hand as easily as if it were a baton, thrusting it forward into Raymond's stomach. Raymond makes a weird gagging noise and bends forward, grabbing his abdomen in pain.

Join the club, I think.

Chris then drops the bar and takes Raymond by the neck.

"I should *kill* you," he growls. His muscles are bulging, his cheeks are flushed. He's angry. *Very* angry.

Raymond gargles an unintelligible response as I cautiously reach out and grab my gun off the ground, tucking it back into my holster.

"Beat it," Chris warns, kicking the now-terrified Raymond forward. "If I see you again, I *will* kill you."

Raymond, still gripping his stomach, nods weakly and takes off across the gas station. I can only stare at Gangster boy's unconscious body strewn atop the asphalt.

Is he dead? I don't want to know.

"Where is it?" Chris asks, breathing hard. He turns to me, pupils dilated. Looks like I'm not the only one who got an adrenaline rush.

"Chris...where's *what*?" I stammer.

"Where'd he *hit* you, Cassie?" he demands. "Did he hit you in the head? Yes or no?"

"What? No." I grimace. "My side, though. It hurts."

Chris swears and lifts my jacket. He pulls the shirt up and I peer down at the skin right above my hip. It's turning black and blue right in front of my eyes. He curses yet again.

He says, "I'm sorry, Cassie."

His voice is gentler than his demeanor. Our eyes meet. I inhale sharply. What's wrong with me? I run my hand through my hair. Chris threads his fingers through mine and brings my hand back down. "Cassie," he says, his voice rough.

I look back up. Raw emotion is burning in his eyes.

"We have to get out of here," I whisper. "There'll be more like them."

Chris nods slowly.

He tucks a strand of hair behind my ear and draws me closer. For a single moment I think that he's going to kiss me. Right here, right now.

Instead, he slips his arm behind my back and leads me to the car. I am capable of walking, but he refuses to let go of me.

"I didn't find any gas," he says, sliding his arms underneath my legs. He lowers me onto the seat, pulling away slowly. My pulse is pounding – more from his touch than from the traumatic attack.

"We'll just have to go as far as we can on what we have, then," I reply. "We'll siphon gas when need to. Right now we need to get out of here."

He rubs his chin. Closes the door. Walks around the Mustang and gets into the driver's seat.

"I'm sorry they hurt you, Cassie," he says. He swallows. Then, "I won't let that happen again. I promise."

I smile despite everything.

"Thanks," I reply softly. "For saving me."

He doesn't answer. He just moves his hand toward the ignition, looking for the keys. "Cassie...?"

I grin.

"Oh, I have them," I say. "I didn't want them to drive off and steal the car."

I reach down into my shirt and take the keys out, tossing them to Chris. He stares at me, then at the keys, then back at me. A self-satisfied smirk touches his lips. "*That's* good to know," he says.

"What's good to know?"

"Where you hide your important stuff."

"Shut up."

He starts the engine and takes the Mustang back onto the old road.

"I say we stay away from all cities until further notice," I propose, wincing every time we hit a bump. "When you were inside I got the crank radio to pick up a signal. They were playing an audio loop of the emergency camps set up for refugees. Apparently the whole state is down."

Chris swears.

"The whole *nation* could be down," he mutters. "Worse than I thought."

"At least they have somewhere for people to *go*," I say.

"No," Chris says, his voice sharp. "Those camps will be full of desperate people who need help. We need to avoid those kinds of places."

"Sometimes people need help, Chris," I point out. "There's nothing wrong with that."

"Trust me, I don't think we're going to want their help."

"What's that supposed to mean?"

"Nothing." He shakes his head. "We'll take a closer look at that hit above your hip once we get far enough away from the populated areas."

"It'll be fine," I say. "It's just a bruise."

"It's still worth checking out," he insists. "You could have fractured something."

His hands grip the steering wheel so hard that I'm afraid he's going to pop it right off.

"The President declared a State of Emergency," I tell him.

"No kidding," Chris laughs, releasing a bit of the tension.

I look down at my hands. They won't stop shaking.

"It's a cabin," I say, closing my eyes.

"Excuse me?"

"The place I'm meeting my dad," I explain. "It's a little cabin we own. We have it stocked with supplies. You...you're welcome to come if you want."

"I have to find my family first."

"After you find your family, then," I say. "My dad says strength is in numbers, anyway."

Chris cocks his eyebrow.

"True." He looks over at me, ghosting a sexy smile. "Thanks for offering."

I blush and turn back toward the window.

Chris?" I ask. "Do you think my dad is still alive?"

There. I said it.

Who's to say that my dad wasn't caught in one of the random explosions in Los Angeles? The odds certainly aren't in his favor.

Chris remains silent for a long time before answering.

"What do *you* believe?" he says at last, glancing at me.

I hesitate.

"I don't know," I answer honestly. "He didn't have the Mustang, so I don't know how he would have got out of the city. The only thing I *do* know is that he'll know exactly where I'm going, and if anyone can make it there alive, it's my father."

Chris gently touches my hand. We lock eyes again.

"Hey," he says. "If your dad is *anything* like you, he's definitely alive."

I bite my lip. Unable to keep my voice steady enough to reply, I smile to convey my thanks. Chris releases my hand and touches my cheek before focusing back on the road.

As we put distance between ourselves and the gas station from hell, I can't help but think how much my life has changed in less than twenty-four hours.

What a trip.

The back roads only go so far. Many of them were abandoned when the government built the current eight-lane interstate. Chris periodically gets out and drags portable fences and "Do Not Enter," obstructions out of the way.

While we've been driving I've been able to dig around my first-aid kit, searching for something to ease the pain of my injury. There's no way to tell if something's broken, so anti-inflammatory cream will have to cover it for now.

Since we left the gas station behind we haven't been able to get another signal on the crank radio. It could be because we're getting higher up into the Grapevine. Radio signals tend to go dead in the hills.

Still...

The old road we're on right now has virtually eroded into mere dirt. Bushes are sometimes overgrown across the road. As we ascend the air gets colder. I spot powdery snow dusting the top of some of the higher mountains. Chris voiced his concern earlier about running out of gas sooner than we had estimated – all of this steep climbing and detouring is costing us mileage.

"When we run out," I say, hating to use the word *when*, "what then?"

Chris ponders the question, avoiding a fallen branch in the road. "We can siphon gas from the cars along the road," he says. "That's what we said we'd do."

"It might be raining or snowing up in the mountains," I point out. "What if the car breaks down?"

"And that's supposed to be worse than staying in the city and getting mugged to death?" Chris says, raising an eyebrow. "Relax, Cassie. I can repair the car if it stops working. And when we run out of gas, I'll find more. We're covered."

"Fine," I sigh. "I just hope the car makes it to Squaw Valley, at least. It's almost forty miles away from our cabin. *And* uphill."

"You could hike it." Chris flicks the radio on again. Still nothing. "Just follow the road and stay out of sight."

"Do you think everyone in the state has gone crazy?" I ask. "Have they all gone psycho?"

"Of course not," Chris replies, smiling. "But the majority don't know how to survive without technology – without electricity or plumbing – and they'll panic. They'll get their hands on anything that works. Upstanding citizens will become criminals in a week or two. Desperation brings human beings down to the same level." His body tightens. "Trust me. I've seen it before."

His voice becomes depressing, dark, and he stops speaking.

I wonder what he's seen. And where.

When nighttime comes we have to refill the gas tank again. That leaves us with about two more gas cans, but with small containers and an old car, that doesn't mean we can get all the way to Squaw

Valley without running out. Thank God Chris knows how to siphon gas from other cars.

Why didn't my dad ever teach me how to do that?

"Chris," I say at around nine o'clock. "We should stop and rest. Both of us."

"We're making good time."

"We're *lost*."

And it's true. We've been driving around the back roads all day. Going on an interstate at eighty miles per hour, it only takes about sixty minutes to get through the Grapevine. It's taken us twelve hours to even get *close*, because many of the roads we've used have been dead ends and we've had to backtrack.

"Cassie…"

"It's insane for us to waste gas driving around in the dark!" I exclaim. "None of my maps have any information about these roads. We need to wait until morning and figure out what's going on. I have no idea what direction we're headed."

Rainclouds have darkened the sky, obscuring the moon and stars. It's getting colder and windier by the minute. The entire windshield is coated with sleet. The climate control system in the Mustang broke about four months ago, and thanks to my habit of procrastination, I never got it fixed. Now I have no heater.

Lovely.

"I don't want the engine to get frozen," Chris mutters. "A car this old might have trouble starting up again."

"I'd rather take that chance and not drive off a cliff," I say.

Chris nods.

"Okay," he replies. "We'll stop and rest for a couple of hours. If it's a full blown winter storm we'll want to keep moving, though."

He's right, of course. Mudslides are pretty common up on the Grapevine during storms. So is flooding and icy roads. It's not like my Mustang is tricked out for that kind of crazy terrain, so it'd be safer not to push it.

Chris finds a spot off the road, wedged between a wall of bushes and trees. He cuts the engine, plunging us into total darkness. I instinctively check all the locks on the car before reaching for my backpack.

"It couldn't get any colder, could it?" I mumble.

I dig through my pack in the dark. I finally find what I'm looking for, a wool camping blanket. I unroll it and spread it over my body. "Cold?" I ask, offering a corner up to Chris.

He shakes his head, instead shrugging on his leather jacket. Even in the dim lighting I could easily imagine him as a sexy greaser from way back when. His hair might be a little long, but still...

"How's your arm?" I ask.

"Fine," he shrugs.

"I should check it to make sure it's not infected."

"It's not infected, Cassie," he grins. "Get some sleep. You're going to need it."

I don't argue. I yawn and curl up, leaning my head against the window. The temperature continues to drop. I pray that the engine doesn't freeze. That we can enjoy a few hours of rest.

The two of us doze off. I glance at the crank radio to check the time, noting that it's only midnight. We've been asleep for three hours. I glance over at Chris, surprised to find him asleep sitting upright against the seat. He looks a lot more relaxed that way. More natural. More handsome.

I flex my fingers. They're freezing, numb. Alarmed, I pull my blanket tighter around my shoulders and lean across the seat. I brush my fingers lightly against Chris's cheek. He snaps awake and grabs my wrist, pinning it against the dashboard. In that moment I can see the pure instinct in his eyes. The natural, unhesitating reaction of military training.

We stare at each other for a few beats.

"What time is it?" he asks, dropping my wrist.

I can't help but notice that *his* hands are warm.

"Midnight," I say, shivering. "It's freaking *cold* up here."

"It's only going to get colder," Chris replies, turning the key in the ignition. It takes the car a few turns to rumble to life. "You okay?"

Thank you, God! It's still alive!

My head is pounding.

"Headache," I mumble.

Chris frowns and touches my forehead.

"You don't have a fever," he says.

"I'm not sick," I answer. "I'm tense. The world just ended, remember?"

He flashes an amused smile as we roll out of the bushes, back onto the road. The windows are covered in a fine layer of ice. The road is dusted with ghostly white snow. It's so thin that it's almost like paper. The roads will be slippery.

"Great," I complain. "Snow. Fantastic."

"What did snow ever do to you?"

"It made me cold." I tuck my legs underneath myself. "Aren't you cold?"

"It's just a little snow."

"Let me guess. You've probably walked uphill, barefoot for forty miles in the snow as a Navy SEAL. You're now impervious to cold weather."

Chris releases a rich, pleasant laugh.

"That would have been a cakewalk compared to what I had to do," he says.

"And what *did* you do?" I ask.

"You don't want to know."

"No, I do." I cup my hand around my ear. "I'm *waiting*."

He rubs the back of his head, seemingly uncomfortable.

"Fine," he says. "I trained in San Diego at the Coronado Naval Air Station when I was eighteen. Two hundred boys go in and forty get to go onto the next level of training."

"Only forty?" I ask.

"Only the best get in," he says. There's pride in his voice.

"Have you been overseas?" I ask.

"Many times."

"Where?" I lean forward. "I always wanted to travel."

"I didn't exactly have time to do a lot of sightseeing," he says. "I've been on six tours since my first deployment. Iraq and Afghanistan for the most part." His face darkens. "That was a couple of years ago, though."

"Why did you quit?"

He doesn't answer.

"Now I know why you have long hair," I remark. "It's very *not* military, you know."

"Hey, I like my hair."

"So do I, I'm just saying."

Chris smiles again and I realize how much I *like* seeing him do so. It's a beautiful thing.

I shiver dramatically and curl up tighter on the seat.

Chris laughs.

"What's so funny?" I demand.

"You haven't been in snow much, have you?" he asks, rolling his eyes.

"No," I huff. "Now I know why. It sucks."

"Nah. It's just different than what you're used to." He shrugs. "Then again, you *are* a city girl."

I mutter something about him about being egotistical before rubbing my hands together. My head hurts *so* bad. I grit my teeth and wrap my fingers around the roots of my hair at the crown. I pull on the hair enough to ease the pain in my head – a trick I learned from reading one too many health forums on the Internet.

The Internet. Now a thing of the past.

"Are you sure you're okay?" he asks again.

"My head hurts," I say. "I think I have some pain meds in my backpack." The pain is intense. It hurts to blink. By the time I rifle through the survival crap in my bag I am tearing the pain medication package open like someone possessed.

"Aren't those children's painkillers?" Chris remarks, seeing the happy face on the label.

"Yes," I groan, chewing the tablet.

"Why not just buy the adult doses? It's more effective."

"I prefer the grape flavor."

He cocks an eyebrow.

"Fine," I confess. "I *like* the happy face on the label. Geez."

Chris bursts into laughter. Whatever. My head hurts and yeah, I *like* the happy face. I fling the bottle back into to the bag. I press my forehead against the freezing window, hoping it will act as the equivalent of an ice pack.

"I'm just going to rest for a minute," I murmur.

I drop off to sleep after a few minutes. I have nightmares about driving down a road that never ends. Ironic. When I wake up it's around three in the morning. Still dark. Still cold.

Still miserable.

"Where are we?" I ask, yawning.

My head feels better. Chris looks weary from driving. I consider offering to take his place, but think better of it. Chris has by far proven himself the better driver of the two of us.

"We're almost to the valley," Chris says. "I think."

"You think?" I blink a few times to focus. "Or are we lost again?"

"We were never *lost*," Chris replies firmly. "We just ran into bad roads."

"We were lost."

"We weren't *lost*."

"Why can't men ever admit it when they're lost?" I lean forward, straining to see out the sleet-covered windshield. "Chris, that's the Interstate."

The narrow back road curves up alongside the mountain and drops off underneath the freeway. Thanks to the EMP, there's not a single pair of headlights in sight.

"The freeway's sloping downhill," I remark. "We *are* getting closer to the valley."

"You wanna chance getting on the Interstate?" Chris asks.

"I don't know," I say. "What about all the dead cars?"

"There's no other road," he replies. "We don't really have a choice. We're far enough away from the city that we might be able to squeeze by the messy areas because traffic here wasn't as dense when the pulse hit."

I shudder, realizing how we've started talking about the "pulse" like it's some *thing*. Some historic event that occurred a hundred years ago.

It was only yesterday.

"Okay," I agree. "But what if there's people?"

"Then we deal with them."

"And what if they get violent?"

"We defend ourselves." He slows the car near the freeway onramp, both of us noting the vehicles lined up on the road. Frozen in time. "We don't have a choice, Cassie. We need to get out of here. The weather will only get worse, and even though *I* might be able to handle the climate, you won't like it."

I sigh, knowing he's right.

"Just keep your gun ready," I advise. A half joke. "I'm ready to shoot anybody who comes too close."

"Right between the eyes?" Chris chuckles, easing onto the freeway.

"Yeah. Right between the eyes."

We move cautiously, picking our way through small pileups and vehicles positioned at odd angles along the highway. As we descend, I search for a glimpse of the Central Valley. Usually I would be able to see a few lights twinkling below but tonight there is nothing but darkness.

Everything's dead. *People* are dead.

"Holy *crap!*" I exclaim.

An oilrig is sitting on its side. The cab window is shattered. Thick smears of blood have dried along the driver door. Some of the liquid from the rig is leaking onto the road, a nasty explosion waiting to happen.

I shut my eyes as we zip past.

This is a bad dream. Wake up, Cassidy.

It's slow going, weaving our way through the wreckage. At one point, we reach a wall of cars. It seems to be stretching from one end of the Interstate to the other. Chris studies it, finds a hole, and deftly maneuvers the Mustang into the pocket.

I'm impressed.

"Chris! I see it!" I cry, lifting myself off the seat.

Relief. Sweet relief.

We've escaped the Grapevine.

Although there is no sign of electricity in the valley, I can easily identify the flat stretch of land peeking out beneath the Tehachapi Mountains.

I clap my hands together.

"Aren't you just a *little* bit relieved?" I ask, shaking my head.

"Yeah." He raises both eyebrows. "But I'm not sure if you are."

I lightly punch him in the shoulder.

"Shut up."

Crash. Something slams against my window. I scream. The whole car shakes with the blunt force of the impact. Chris hits the gas and the Mustang lurches forward. I see dark shapes. Humans. They're running through the spaces between the dead cars. They flit by like shadows, flashes of arms, legs, and faces.

"Chris!"

"I see them."

We don't stop. We can't. I catch a glimpse of a man wearing an orange construction vest. Our headlights light up his clothes like a beacon.

He's standing in the middle of the road.

"Chris...!" I shout. "He's not moving!"

More shadows. More movement.

"We're not stopping," Chris replies.

"But Chris -"

The construction worker is close. Closer.

He stares at us. Perhaps trying to scare us. To get us to stop. That is, after all, how Chris got me to stop *my* car and pick *him* up. But this is different. There are far too many people outside to stop. We aren't alone.

He barely steps to the side, but not far enough out of the way. His leg catches on the front fender of the Mustang, spinning him through the air. He hits the pavement with a sickening thud. I grip the door handle, shocked. Chris doesn't react. He continues to drive as if nothing happened.

Always focused.

How long have these people been stuck out here, waiting for emergency assistance that never came? How *many* of them are there?

"Hit the gas!" I yell.

Chris floors it as much as he dares. People continue to slam against the side of the Mustang in an attempt to grab onto the roof or trunk.

Chris dodges stragglers without too much difficulty but the car pileups are getting bigger.

"Chris..." I whisper, fear slithering down my spine.

There is a massive car accident in front of us. A semi truck is lying on its side, blocking half the road. Other vehicles are stacked on the opposite end, completely barricading the freeway.

"Turn around!" I say. "We have to get out of here!"

"I'm doing the best I can," Chris replies, irritated.

He swings the car into a quick U-turn. The headlights illuminate the road. I stare.

Oh, God. Save us.

A mob of people is moving toward us. Climbing over cars, clawing their way over the barriers on the freeway. Some of them are bloody. Others are dressed in clean clothes. The desperation emanating from the mob is palpable, visible in their eyes. Thick in the air. They're coming from all sides. We have nowhere to go but *into* the mob if we want to escape.

"Get your pack," Chris warns. "Get everything you can."

"But-"

"-Just *do* it!"

I strap my backpack on and grab the one that belongs to Chris. Chris doesn't stop the car but keeps moving forward as three people climb onto the trunk. They bang on the windows, shrieking profanities. Scared, trembling, I look to Chris, hoping he'll offer a solution. But what can he do? People are throwing themselves at the car, creating a human barrier around the entire vehicle. Soon the human load is so heavy that Chris can't move the car forward. The banging and yelling gets more intense. The windows begin to crack.

I look around frantically, searching for an escape.

No escape. Trapped again! What now?

At last one of the rioters breaks through the passenger window. They rip more of the glass away with their bare hands. Blood drips down their fingers as the glass tears away pieces of their flesh.

"Cassidy!" Chris shouts. Rioters break the glass in the driver window. More hands enter the cab. Arms reach through the window, grabbing my hair, head, shoulders, waist. Dragging me outside. I yell and kick, biting and clawing at a writhing mass of arms and legs. I feel Chris's hand on my ankle as he tries to yank me back inside the car, but really – what good would that do?

We've been caught in a swarm.

I'm pulled into the night air, sucked into a swirling mob of people, crushed in on all sides. Sweaty, bloody bodies are everywhere. Boxing me in. I can't breathe, I can *barely* see and the mob is breaking more of the windows on the Mustang.

They're destroying it.

A group of stragglers attempt to rip my backpack off my shoulders. It's strapped on at two places: across my chest and across my waist. I hold onto it for dear life. What I have in this backpack is far more valuable than the Mustang.

"Give us the pack!" A woman wearing a white, stained pencil skirt grabs my face, shoving it close to hers. "Give it to us!" she screams. Blood is dribbling out the side of her mouth. Horrified, I shove her away and she is swallowed into the gaping maw of the crowd.

"Take the car!" someone cries. The mob surges forward, getting tighter, wilder. Some are wearing beachwear, others are wearing professional attire. I notice burned faces and raw flesh. Black and blue bruises and torn clothing.

These people are desperate. Insane with terror.

"Give me the girl!" Chris shouts.

His voice is loud and clear. Commanding.

I spot him climbing onto the roof of the Mustang. He's got his backpack on one shoulder – a miracle – and his semi-automatic weapon in the other hand. The crowd doesn't pay him any attention.

Until he shoots.

He points his handgun at the sky and fires off a round. The sound draws everybody's attention. It's as if an instant freeze falls over the crowd.

"Give me the girl," Chris commands, his voice echoing over the scene of destruction. "Or I will kill as many people as I can before I'm done."

Wise choice of words. Because no matter how insane these people are, the fact is that they want to *survive*. Being shot will take that away. Instantly.

The crowd surrounding me parts just enough for me to work my way back to the Mustang. Chris keeps the gun in plain sight, his free hand up in the air. He jumps down on the asphalt and hooks his arm around my waist. I hang onto him for all I'm worth as we push through the mob, people backing off a few feet.

When we clear the crowd, there is a moment where the two of us stare at the mob, and they return the gaze. Chris keeps his weapon trained on the group. Everyone slowly returns their attention to the Mustang, and we are soon forgotten.

We are not what they want.

"Chris, my gun is in the car!" I say, feeling my empty holster. "I took it out..."

Chris grabs my hand and yanks me away.

"Move," he commands. "Now."

"My *car*," I moan.

We break into a jog, putting distance between us and the mob from the mouth of hell. Chris climbs up the side of the overturned semi and reaches down for me. I take his hands and he pulls me up just as another gunshot rings through the air. People in the mob disperse and break for the hills. The Mustang rolls forward. I hear the engine rev to life. The vehicle lurches backward and forward as people cram their bodies into the tiny cab, trying to steal the car for themselves.

It's painful to watch.

But we have to leave. Or we will be killed.

Chris drops to the ground and holds out his arms for me. I jump down, wincing from my injury. Chris catches me around the waist, his fingers lightly grazing my bruised hip. A ribbon of blood runs down his forehead.

"Are you okay?" I ask.

Stupid question. We're *so* not okay.

Chris offers a soft smile, touching my cheek.

"Are you?"

I nod.

"Let's move, then," he says.

I pause, another crash breaking the silence of the night.

"What are we going to do without the car?" I ask.

I feel exposed and unprotected without it.

"We'll be okay," Chris replies. "We've got our packs."

He starts walking down the freeway. I swallow thickly. Hot tears slide down my cheeks. I stumble to catch up with him, crying silently. Not because a bunch of losers just wrecked our only form of transportation, or because our gas supply was stolen, or because our water is gone. But because this is what the world has been reduced to in less than forty-eight hours after the pulse hit.

It sucks. Big time.

Chapter Five

My dad used to tell me:

"Life is hard, and then you die."

Yeah. He wasn't the optimistic type.

Mom was. She was into Eastern religion. Every day before school I would find her sitting motionless in the living room, focusing on meditation. She was in love with the idea of Nirvana and self-discovery. Eternal optimism. Being one with nature. Reincarnation. All that stuff.

As for myself? I tended to side with Dad's philosophy: Try and survive while you're here, because life is short and tough.

Maybe if I had known *how* tough things were going to be I would have built a bulletproof motorhome and stocked it with artillery and food. That way I wouldn't be in my present situation.

Which is very, very tough.

Dawn is breaking over the horizon, turning the landscape to a faded blue. The sky is covered with a canopy of angry rainclouds. And by angry, I mean *furious*. They're dark, heavy. Ready to let loose.

We have followed the freeway and now we're standing at the beginning of a huge bridge that slopes down to the valley. Chris is hauling his backpack like it weighs nothing. It must be nice being six foot four and all muscle. I'm only two inches above five feet and comparing my muscle mass to his is like setting a grizzly bear and a rabbit side by side.

It's not happening.

"The rest stop is no more than an hour away," Chris says, pausing at the top of the slope. "Can you make it?"

I trudge forward to keep pace, tight with cold. There's a large rest stop at the bottom of the hill. There aren't any lights. It's impossible to tell from here if there's any human activity.

"Yeah, of course," I retort, insulted. "I'm not *that* weak."

Chris assesses my drooping posture and heavy breathing.

"Whatever you say," he shrugs.

As we walk downhill I note the presence of runaway truck ramps. Semis are piled up here more than anywhere previously on the road.

"I'm glad I wasn't driving when it hit," I state.

Chris makes a sound in the back of his throat, reminding me that he *was* driving when the EMP hit. A motorcycle, no less.

" So... do you do a lot of biking?" I ask, trying to make small talk.

He nods.

"I've never been on a bike," I say. "I mean, I've been on a *bike* but not a motorcycle."

"And why is that?" he asks.

"Bugs. They get in your mouth, right? That's just gross."

Chris makes a face.

"If you ride around with your mouth hanging open, I assume that could be a possibility."

"Well, unless you wear a helmet," I point out.

"Helmets aren't always comfortable."

"Why? Do they ruin your perfect hair?" I tug on my waist-length locks. "I don't know if I'd be able to fit all this into a helmet, anyway."

60

In an act of uncharacteristic playfulness, Chris steps to the side and tugs on the ends of my hair.

"Hey, knock it off!" I laugh.

"You're like Rapunzel," he says, threading his fingers through the long locks. "A ginger Rapunzel, actually."

"Who says Rapunzel couldn't be a redhead?"

"I don't know. Who said?"

He swings around and blocks my path. I bump against his chest, his arms coming up around my waist.

"What do you think you're *doing*?" I demand.

"Nothing," Chris says, raising an eyebrow. Staring at me with those electric green eyes. "Just messing with you, kid."

He uses both hands to comb the hair back from my face. My arms prickle with goose bumps. He rests his thumbs against my cheeks and we stand there, staring at each other in silence. He seems to be searching my expression for something, some kind of secret signal, as he leans forward, closer.

The tip of his nose touches mine. Right then it becomes painfully obvious *exactly* what's about to happen. I step backwards and twist out of his arms, pretending to adjust my backpack. My face is hot, tingling with a rush of warm blood. My heart beats quickly, hyperaware of even the soft touch of fabric against my skin.

"We'd better move faster," I say, breathless, avoiding his eyes. "Maybe we can find shelter before it starts to rain."

Chris turns around, his face showing only a hint of irritation. He nods, wordless, and we set off together, the most uncomfortable silence in history hanging between the two of us.

I push the almost-kiss thing out of my mind and stare at the rest stop in the distance. It will be my goal of the moment. My focus. Maybe Chris feels the same way, because he seems determined to leave me in his dust as he walks along, making a point of staying in front.

Men.

It takes us an hour to walk down the massive freeway slope. It makes me appreciate that much more the awesomeness of cars. And trains. And planes. And bicycles. At the bottom there's an empty restaurant. No cars. No people.

I blink. An odd feeling takes hold of me. I saw a scene like this in a movie once. A zombie movie. A farmer walked into town, realizing too late that there was no human life left...only the undead. The remainder of the film was spent watching him take out walking corpses with a pitchfork.

While the zombie part is completely ludicrous, *this* is not. There are no humans. Anywhere. No signs of life. Nothing but sheer abandonment and empty space. There should be at least *some* military vehicles like the National Guard coming in to help with a crisis like this.

Not every single vehicle in the military is gone. Are they?

Or is the entire country down?

And if so, who did it?

And what purpose was behind it?

I push the thoughts away and focus on the rest stop. There are four restaurants, three gas stations and a handful of fast food chains.

"Do you think it's safe?" I ask, voicing the obvious question.

Chris doesn't answer for a long time.

Finally he says, "I doubt it."

"Then we should bypass it."

"No. We need to rest and a storm's coming up. We need shelter."

Right. Wasn't *I* the one who said that very thing just a little bit ago? Men will be men. I keep my mouth shut. We reach the rest stop a half an hour later. There are cars everywhere, though the ones here don't appear nearly as ravaged as the ones on the Grapevine. Still no signs of life. We take the off ramp.

The lack of background noise is unsettling.

No jets. No cars. No conversations. No text alerts.

"This is unusual," Chris says.

I stare at him.

"You *think*?"

We walk across the freeway overpass. I gasp. There is blood on the guardrails. It's not a lot of blood, but it's splattered on the sidewalk in a long, uneven line.

"Chris..." I murmur.

He kneels down, studying the pavement. His looks up at me, his expression dark. "I've seen this before," he says.

"You've seen *this*?"

A cold sensation squeezes my chest.

What does *that* mean?

Chris sets his jaw and walks forward. This time his handgun is in plain sight. It makes me nervous. He wouldn't take it out unless he thought we were in danger. I swallow and walk in his footsteps, staying behind his shoulder. As we come over the end of the overpass, I find myself struggling to breathe. A horrified scream sticks in my throat as I look out over the four-lane boulevard leading into the rest area.

It's covered with bodies.

Hundreds. They're strewn out in uneven patches, some stacked on top of each other. The stench from the drying blood is so strong that it permeates everything – including me. I run to the guardrail and puke over the side.

It's sickening. It's unimaginable.

It can't be real.

"What the hell...?" Chris says, lowering his weapon.

I look down at my feet and notice something else. The pavement is streaked with the same sticky blood that covered the sidewalk on the overpass.

Chris suddenly turns to me, a look of hard anger on his face.

"This is no accident," he states.

I stare, knowing that I'm shaking like a leaf.

"Cassidy," he says. His voice is gentler. "Look at me."

But I can't. I'm smelling the blood, seeing the blood, looking at the bodies lined up - no, *piled* – on the boulevard. I can't pull my eyes away. I can't stop *looking*.

Chris places his hands on my shoulders.

"Look. At. Me." It's not a request.

I barely manage to lift my eyes to meet his – and they're not quite as emotionless as I would have expected. Instead, his expression is soft. "Say something, kid," he says, stroking my cheek. "Look at me."

"What happened?" I say, monotone.

He searches my face for a long time before turning me around. He laces his fingers through mine and pulls me forward, purpose in each step.

"Where are we going?" I stutter, numb.

"Whatever happened here," Chris says, shoving a few loose strands of hair away from his face, "was not an accident. It was a systematic extermination."

"Who would do this?"

He shrugs. Obviously neither of us can answer that one, but chances are that whoever did this was a part of the same group of sick minds that hit our world with an EMP.

"What about shelter?" I say.

"Not here. This blood is fresh. This didn't happen more than twenty-four hours ago," Chris points out. "Look at this trail of blood. People were *lined* up and executed."

I breathe faster.

"Oh, my God." I cover my mouth with my hand, more food coming up my throat. "Is this a nightmare? This isn't real, right?"

Chris rubs his chin, assessing my condition.

"This is real," he says at last. Firm. "And we're going to be okay. Got that?"

I nod, numb.

He takes my hand again and we leave via the freeway onramp. I notice how the buildings along the interstate have broken windows. Some of the glass is black – like it may have burned from within. The freeway is also covered with thick black marks. Not tire marks. Something else.

What's going on? This is America.

Things like this?

They just don't happen.

Chapter Six

Sometime after dark, the storm hits. I've stopped keeping track of time. It's useless when you're dragging yourself down mile after mile of bland interstate. Time becomes meaningless. Day and night blurs together.

Chris and I take shelter in an abandoned SUV on the side of the road. The back seat folds down, giving us plenty of room to stretch out. We crawl inside, dripping on the upholstery. A basket of baby toys sits on the floor. How sad.

I wonder what happened to the passengers in this car.

Pit pat, pit pat. The raindrops are loud without constant background noise. I sit with my knees against my chest, cold, wet and hungry. Chris looks unhappy as he shrugs off his leather jacket. The fabric has been ruined by the weather. After a few minutes of sitting in silence he finally says,

"There's an explanation."

I blink.

"What?"

"Those bodies," he continues. "There's an explanation for how they got there."

"Of course there is. I just don't want to think about it." I comb back my sopping hair with my fingers. "It obviously wasn't *our* side."

Chris doesn't answer.

"I mean, it *wasn't* our side, right?" I press.

"How should I know?"

"You were in the military, that's why!" I exclaim. "You should know these things. My *dad* would."

Chris shakes his head.

"I haven't been active duty for a year," he says, propping his head against the backpack. "There's a lot I wouldn't know. I'm not in the loop anymore."

"You're real helpful, aren't you?" I make a face.

Chris declines to fling a sarcastic remark back at me. I'm disappointed.

I mean, he could at least *try*.

I unroll the camping blanket from my backpack and spread it over my legs, conserving what little warmth there is. I doubt there's any heat left on this side of the planet, though. It got sucked out with people's sanity forty-eight hours ago.

Forty-eight hours. Is that all it's been?

I curl up in a tight ball, only a foot of space between Chris and me. This would be awkward, but for the most part, I don't care. I'm too *tired* to waste my time thinking about it.

Chris falls asleep almost instantly. I suppose after nine years of being a Navy SEAL, he can sleep through anything – even the end of the world. It takes me longer to relax. When I finally drop off I have terrifying dreams about the hundreds of bloody corpses we found at the rest stop. I force myself awake.

I'm surprised to find that it's already early morning. It's still raining, unfortunately. I curse the rain gods and make a move to sit up. Something heavy is draped around my waist.

68

Chris's arms are wrapped around me, pressing my back against his chest. No wonder I was so warm. Embarrassed, I lower myself down and pretend I'm asleep as he stirs. I don't want to be awake when he realizes he and I had a cuddle fest. All night.

Awkward...

"Cassie?" he whispers, shifting. "What time is it?"

I freeze, keeping my eyes squeezed shut.

"I know you're awake," he continues, lifting himself up on one arm. "Don't deny it."

I roll my eyes.

"I just woke up. And you can let go."

"Why? Aren't you warm?" He smiles against my ear, keeping his grip firm.

"No," I swallow, extricating myself from his embrace.

"I did it for you," he smirks, shaking his hair out of his ponytail. "I thought you'd appreciate *not* freezing to death during the night."

"Whatever," I say. "You don't have to be weird about it."

"I'm not the one being weird about it. You are."

I shoot him my most menacing glare before rolling up my blanket. I stuff it into my backpack with force. Not because I'm mad at *him* for cozying up to me during the night, but because I *liked* the way it felt.

I shouldn't be feeling those kinds of emotions.

I should be worried about survival.

I zip my pack up and take a look around the freeway through the tinted windows of the SUV. There's still not a soul in sight. Only miles of abandoned cars and a canopy of rainclouds.

"Exactly *how* are we supposed to get to Squaw Valley on foot?" I say, giving voice to the thought that has been at the forefront of my mind ever since we lost my Mustang. "Because that could be a *long* stroll in this weather. Besides, I don't even think I have enough food in my pack to last that long."

"It's about two hundred miles away, right?" Chris replies.

"I guess."

"I'd say if we keep walking every day and make good time, it could take…" he pauses and thinks it over. "Maybe two weeks. If we can do about fifteen miles a day."

"Do I *look* like a marathon runner to you?" I say, frowning. "I don't even lift weights."

Chris flashes a smug grin.

"Thankfully, I'm in *great* shape, so if you collapse with exhaustion, I'll be more than happy to carry you all the way there."

"Sure you will," I mumble. "And then what are you going to do? Bug out with your little brother and leave me in the middle of the wilderness?"

He raises his eyebrows.

"What happens, happens," he says.

I open my mouth to say something sarcastic and brilliant before I close it again. I don't have to reply. Saying nothing is often better saying something I'll regret, anyway.

Not that I have a great track record of keeping my mouth shut.

"Ease up, kid," he advises, pulling his tee shirt off. "We've got a long way to go and you're going to want to stick with me."

I press my back against the interior of the trunk and stare, his muscular upper body taking center stage in my brain. Wow.

Just...wow.

He says something.

"What?" I reply, absent.

"Forget it," Chris replies.

He's smiling cunningly.

A tattoo of a vicious cobra winds around his left bicep. He's also wearing a gold chain around his neck. "See something of interest?" he asks, raising an eyebrow.

I clear my throat.

"No. Put a shirt on, will you? It's not polite," I say, popping the trunk to the SUV open. The cold air is refreshing. My heart rate slows. I close my eyes, regain control of my jumbled emotions and ask,

"How's your arm doing?"

"Fine," he says. "It's healing up."

Chris hops out of the vehicle, wearing a tight black tee, every muscle in his arms and chest on display. He pulls his hair back and throws his backpack over his shoulder. He looks scary.

Or maybe that's his happy face.

"You got any breakfast in that magic pack of yours?" he asks, nodding at my backpack.

"A little." I unzip the top, pulling out a high-nutrient protein bar. We split it just as the rain subsides a bit. "Tastes kind of like paper."

I chew it slowly, contemplating its dull texture.

"That's probably the crappiest thing I've ever tasted," he remarks. "Then again...in comparison to insects, maybe not."

"You've eaten *bugs*?"

He nods.

"Intentionally?" I ask.

"For training." He grins. "*And* I was hungry."

I shake my head.

"You really *are* insane." I spread my hands apart. "Well, fearless leader, shall we begin our long march toward destiny?"

Chris looks slightly annoyed.

"Yeah. Why not?"

And so we begin a boring, flat, wet, cold, miserable and bleak walk across an abandoned interstate. As we progress, the fact that there are *no* people *anywhere* continually eats at my nerves. Something is horribly wrong.

Are there more dead bodies hidden alongside the freeway?

"Chris?" I ask. "Do you think we're being invaded?"

To my surprise, he doesn't laugh. Instead he thinks it over before answering, "It's possible. But how could an army invade so quickly, kill a huge number of civilians, and then disappear? Where are their vehicles? Why aren't we seeing them out in the open?" He stops and sighs, frustrated. "The whole damn thing doesn't make any sense."

I agree. An EMP, a pile of bloody corpses at the rest stop...maybe *that's* why all the people who mobbed us in the Mustang were so freaked out. Maybe they'd seen something. Something bad. Something that had to do with the bodies at the rest stop.

Something that made them wild with desperation.

"I don't know what to think," I say. "My dad always believed that a natural disaster or nuclear bomb was what we were supposed to be prepared for. But this is *not* what I had in mind."

"It took everyone by surprise," Chris replies.

The rain falls harder. The only thing I have going for me is my waterproof jacket, but I'm still cold enough to freeze upright.

"I'm going to need more water," I say. "I'm getting dehydrated."

"Open your mouth," he advises. "It *is* raining."

"Yeah, I noticed that." I stick my tongue out, catching a few raindrops. "Hey, we should try the radio again. Maybe we'll get a signal down here."

Chris shrugs.

"Go ahead."

I stop and pull the radio out of my backpack. It's waterproof, so the rain won't ruin it. After a few minutes of cranking – and wondering why Chris doesn't offer to do it since he has muscles the size of tree trunks – I flip the radio on.

The first three stations are dead – not even static. The fourth one has a flickering voice we can't make out. The fifth one is a recitation of the same audio loop I heard up at the gas station in Santa Clarita. Emergency camps in Elk Grove, Bakersfield, San Jose, Fresno, etc.

I turn it off.

"Great. All the radio stations are down," I say.

"They're just looping the same audio," Chris answers. "Which means there's nobody there anymore. As soon as the emergency broadcast center loses power is, the loop will stop."

"That's cheery news."

I shove the radio back into my pack, disappointed. I'd hoped to hear a radio announcer saying something like,

"Check it out, folks! The world is back to normal. You can all come home and watch TV now."

Fat chance.

We keep walking. I follow behind Chris, catching raindrops on my tongue to pass the time.

"We're going to run out of food and water before we reach Squaw Valley," I say at last, having avoided the subject for about twenty-four hours. "You know that, right?"

"I know."

"Then we need to stop at one of those emergency camps," I reply. "There's one in Bakersfield. That's only about forty miles from here."

Chris shakes his head.

"No," he says, his voice firm. "Going into a camp like that is *not* a good idea. Besides, there are more than enough grocery stores and restaurants to raid at this point."

"But why not *try* the camps? They'll have supplies. Clean clothes. Real food." I shiver. "And probably space heaters."

"Bad idea," he insists. "The less people know about who we are and where we're going, the better."

"But they can *help* us!"

"No, Cassidy. It's not safe."

I kick a piece of trash across the freeway. He's right. I *know* he's right. I should take his advice. But this situation has stretched my patience to the breaking point.

"Who put you in charge?" I demand. "Last I checked, I'm the one who *gave* you a ride in my Mustang."

"Last I checked, I know more about surviving in war zones than you do," he replies, nonchalant. "Which is pretty much where we find ourselves, little girl."

Little girl?

"You do *not* tell me what to do," I say, angry. "I don't care how many years you were a Navy SEAL. Chris, there might be a way to contact my father at the camp. Maybe they've got phones or radios. You want to bypass it? Fine. I'll go by myself."

He stops, pushing stray hairs out of his face.

"Have it your way," he answers, prowling ahead.

His anger is passive. Simmering, barely visible.

But it's there.

If he doesn't want to cooperate, he doesn't have to.

I'll just be an army of one.

Chapter Seven

Long story short, it takes us about two and a half days to get to Bakersfield. By the time I drag my sorry butt to the other side of the city limit line, I'm willing to take anything – even a *skateboard* – over walking. I'm soaked to the bone, freezing, starving, and the headache I had on the Grapevine is back in full force, slamming against my skull like a sledgehammer.

As for Chris, he and I went for about twenty-four hours without speaking. Well, *I* went without speaking while he carried on one-way conversations.

By this point we are both so hungry and cold that Chris has agreed to scope out the emergency camp – but only on the condition that we don't show ourselves unless we're positive that it's safe.

I don't disagree. After what I've seen, caution is a *must*.

I suppose that, deep down, both of us are holding out hope that the emergency camps might actually be able to help us. That perhaps there's someone who can explain the mass murder we stumbled upon at the rest stop.

We can only hope, after all.

Bakersfield is basically a flat city in the middle of a desert. Today there's not a soul in sight, but I've gotten used to the absence of people over the last four and half days. We take an off ramp into the heart of the city, right where there's a big blue and yellow sign that says *Bakersfield*. The streets are flooded with water. Windows have been punched out of storefronts. The restaurants and grocery stores are ransacked.

On the other side of the freeway, I can see big, open fields. John Wayne's oil fields, Dad would always tell me when we drove through this area on our way to the mountains. Whether or not John Wayne actually drilled for oil here is another story.

"Where is it?" I ask, confused. "Where are all the people?"

"If there's a relief camp here," Chris observes, "it should be near the city center."

He doesn't look too sure.

We follow a curving road that cuts beneath the Bakersfield sign. After a few hundred feet we come to a cluster of hotels and restaurants.

Whoa.

There are *people* everywhere!

Chain link fences surround the entire shopping center, marked with signs that read *EMERGENCY RELIEF CAMP*. Men, women and children are sitting around the edges of the fence, most of them wearing garbage bags to shield themselves from the rain. Military trucks are parked on the asphalt. Officials wearing black uniforms are standing guard around the buildings.

"*This* is an emergency camp?" I say, disbelief flooding through me. "What's up with all the garbage bags?"

"Those are ponchos, actually," Chris corrects, a wry grin on his face. "And don't move. What do you see there?" He points to the outer edge of an old motel. An official is standing next to a soldier in a dark blue uniform. *Both* of them are armed.

"Why are they armed?" I whisper.

We sink into the shadows of the trees, watching the camp through the leaves. "Good question," Chris says.

An elderly woman moves around the parking lot, fenced off and guarded by the black uniformed men. There are stockpiles of supplies there. A few refugees are climbing up and down the outdoor stairwell of the old motels. Others are milling around the fast food restaurants.

"This is...weird," I say.

"This is wrong," he replies. His hands tighten into fists. "Follow me."

I do. Without question.

As far as I can tell, there is no ENTER HERE sign anywhere around the camp, and there's certainly no Red Cross truck.

Something is seriously whacked.

Chris leads me through the park across the street from the relief camp, pausing behind a parked car on the curb. We kneel beside it and, since it's almost nighttime, stand up and approach the fence. My heart beats faster.

Chris turns and follows the curve of the fence, going around the shopping center, ducking behind every other abandoned car on the street. No one notices us. Refugees are staring at the puddles on the ground or sitting motionless with their eyes closed.

Oblivious.

Chris raises his hand and makes a fist, a signal to stop.

I nearly run headlong into his back just as he drops to the ground in a crouch. We're on the other side of the parking lot, looking out over the shopping center. The fence covers a lot more ground than I thought. And the weirdest part? There's no open space. No exit, only a gated entrance with a cadre of armed guards hovering around it. There's also an abundance of wicked-looking barbed wire looped across the top of the fence.

It looks like…

A cage.

"Chris…" I whisper, a chilling thought creeping into my mind.

"I know."

He turns his gaze elsewhere. His jaw hardens and he utters a curse, staring.

"What?" I demand. "What is it?"

He presses his forehead against his hand, taking a deep breath.

I search the parking lot. All I see is are refugees gathered inside the camp. Nearer to us is a pile of supplies covered with white tarpaulin.

"They're *bodies*, Cassie," Chris hisses, turning my chin toward the tarp. "Underneath. Not supplies. Dead bodies."

I suck my breath in. He's right. Red stains can be seen around the corners. Dried blood? I slap my hands over my mouth in order to avoid screaming.

"Oh, God…" I kneel, getting a handle on my breathing. "Why are they collecting them like that? Why don't they just bury them?"

"They'll probably burn them."

I cover my mouth.

I will not gag. I will not cry.

Chris places his hand on the small of my back, smoothing my hair away from my face. He turns my head upward, one hand on each cheek. "We have to get out of here," he whispers. "Can you do that?"

I manage to move my head. A nod.

He takes my hand. His touch calms me, somehow.

We back slowly away from the camp, but Chris stops and makes a motion for me to kneel in the bushes and be quiet.

"Who are these people?" I say, quivering. "What kind of an army does this?"

Chris frowns, wrinkling his brow. Both of us listen to the distant chatter of the conversations between the uniformed men.

"German," he whispers.

"*What?*"

"They're speaking German," he replies. "And if I'm not mistaken..." he pauses, concentrating. "There's a little French in there, too."

"Is this some kind of foreign invasion?" I breathe.

"I don't know." Chris points to the men wearing the dark blue uniforms. There is a black patch on their sleeve, over which is a white O. One of the guards turns around, and I can see a larger insignia stitched on the back of his jacket. It reads: **Omega.** The O is significantly larger than the rest of the lettering, designed to hold a picture of the continents of the world inside the sphere. "I've never seen a uniform like that." He rests his arm on his knee. "What the hell does Omega stand for?" He nods toward the guys in the black. "No insignia. They could be mercenaries."

"Omega could be an acronym," I suggest. "I don't know. Chris, please. Let's get out of here. This was a bad idea."

"Agreed."

But what we don't say is that we *needed* to see this.

We needed to know.

He studies the scene before us for a moment longer before he puts his arm around my shoulders and pulls me down the street, scanning for movement. We reach the Bakersfield sign again and keep walking until we find another freeway onramp.

That's when we hear the noise.

Music.

Chris and I share a glance, surprised. It seems to be echoing down the street. It sounds like pop. "

What's going on?" I whisper, bewildered.

He shakes his head.

We wordlessly follow the sound. We pass a few empty businesses – a loan company and a coffee shop – until we reach the corner. I poke my head around the edge of a brick building and stare.

Generator-powered lights are hooked up to the tops of the buildings. There are civilians here. They are not fenced in, but most of the buildings are covered with odd graffiti. I can't make out what it says; Chris doesn't comment.

Omega troops patrol the sidewalks, identifiable by their blue uniforms. I squint at a fairly new poster that has been taped onto a storefront window. I can't quite make out what it says…

I duck behind a building when a trooper turns his gaze toward the corner. The back of my head presses against a bookstore window. I look up. Another poster is taped here, this time to the outside of the glass. I snatch it up, reading the bold lettering in the dim lighting:

STATE OF EMERGENCY

We are here to help. Please report to the Main Camp in the center of the city. Emergency supplies will be distributed there.

Cooperate and we will survive the collapse.

Confused, I fold it up and stuff it in my pocket just as Chris meets my gaze.

"What?" I whisper.

He shakes his head, motioning for me to follow him. I do.

"What *was* that?" I exclaim. "Because it *sure* wasn't a bunch of people waiting in line for a Black Friday sale."

It's like something you see in the movies, one of those scary films about Nazi Germany. Keeping our backs to the wall of the building, Chris and I exchange glances. This is wrong on *so* many levels.

"We should leave," I whisper.

"No argument there," he replies. "We'll make a…"

His eyes narrow, zeroing in on something across the street. I follow his line of sight. My muscles seize up. A man is standing at the entrance of an alleyway, dressed in khakis and a Hawaiian polo shirt. He's older, with thinning gray hair, a mustache, and round glasses that reflect the harsh floodlights.

He makes a motion to us.

I look at Chris. "What does he want?" I ask.

He answers, "He's a civilian."

I lick my lips, realizing how dry my mouth is. Anxiety.

"So?"

The man motions again. This time he mouths the word, "Help."

Chris immediately takes my arm and sprints across the street. He does it smoothly. Deftly. Without being seen.

We make it across the street, stopping to take cover behind the alley wall. Up close, the man's skin appears ashen. His eyes are watery. "Thank you," he says, his voice rough and weary.

Weary with *what*? Pain? Exhaustion?

"What's going on?" Chris asks.

"What *isn't* going on, son?" he shakes his head. "Look, you kids need to get off the streets. It's too late to be wandering around."

"Too late?" I ask.

"The curfew." The man looks at me like I'm crazy. "You're not local. Am I right?"

"That's correct," Chris says.

"Then why in..." he trails off. "You'd better come with me. If they catch us out here we'll all get punished."

He turns. He walks.

We follow.

He has an obvious limp, and as we walk, I notice purple bruises on the back of his neck and arms. "Can you tell us what's happening here?" I ask. "Why are they killing people? What's –"

The man whips around so fast that I stumble backwards and hit Chris in the chest.

"Keep your mouth shut," he hisses. "You'll get us all killed with questions like that. Just keep your head down and follow me."

Chris wraps his fingers around my elbow and presses a finger against his lips, indicating that we should be silent. "Can we trust him?" I mouth.

Chris shrugs.

Of course not.

We follow the old man down the alley. He pauses where it connects to another street, checking each direction. There doesn't seem to be any Omega guards patrolling the streets. No pop music.

The old man makes a quick right and stays close to a brick apartment building. Trash and food wrappers are littered across the sidewalk. I watch a scruffy dog run into the street, sniff some garbage, and disappear.

The old man stops at an apartment door. It's a heavy wooden thing, protected with metal security bars. He unlocks the bars and the door with a key, ushers us inside, and locks everything behind us.

I keep a firm grip on Chris's arm as we step into a dark, dusty stairwell. The old man says, "Watch your step," and climbs the carpeted steps in front of us. It's impossible to tell how wide the stairway is, or what color the walls are. Chris and I trail behind him until we come to the fourth floor.

We enter a narrow hallway. It reeks of cigarettes. The building is silent. Holes have been burned into the heinous green shag carpet lining the floor. At last, the old man stops in front of an apartment door, opens it, and motions for us to go inside. Chris walks in first, ready to take whatever surprise is waiting for us. I follow the old man inside, surprised to see nothing but a small room illuminated by the light of multiple candles.

No trap.

There are books everywhere, and pictures, too. The old man locks the door behind us, takes a deep breath and says,

"*Now* we can talk." He offers his hand. "The name's Walter Lewis."

Chris shakes his hand.

"Chris," he replies, leaving out his last name. "And this is Cassidy."

Walter turns to look at me.

"You together?" he asks.

I shift uncomfortably. Chris, however, has no qualms.

"Technically," Chris replies. "But I think you owe us an explanation first. Who are you and why did you bring us here?"

*Technically? What does **that** mean?*

Walter wipes his hands on his pants.

"You were out past curfew," he says. "You could have been shot."

He walks past me and disappears through a door, popping up on the other side of a short wall. I take a step back. He's standing over the kitchen sink, looking into the living room. The curtains are pulled tight over the windows – nailed, actually.

"What curfew?" I ask. "Do you know anything about these camps? Where are those soldiers from? They were speaking all these languages..."

Walter sighs and I hear him pouring water into something metal. When he comes back into the living room, he's holding a coffeepot and some mugs.

"They – meaning Omega - arrived here the day after the EMP destroyed everything," he says, setting the mugs on a coffee table crowded with magazines. "Started rounding people up, sending them to the Emergency Relief Camp – that's what they called it at the beginning." His eyes become hooded, sad. "Most people went willingly."

He pours coffee into the mugs and offers a cup to each of us. I whisper thanks and close my hands around the hot glass. "Why are they killing people? Who's Omega? I've never heard of them."

Walter looks long and hard at me.

"Truthfully, I'm not really sure," he says at last. "It's merely the name they've chosen to give to us: Omega."

"Where do they come from?"

"I've never heard of them either," Chris replies. He looks completely puzzled. And here I thought he knew everything. "What do you know about what's happened?"

I look back at Walter for a deeper analysis.

"Your name is Cassidy, isn't it?" he asks, furrowing his brow.

"Yeah," I say.

He strokes his chin, setting the coffeepot down and rifling through a stack of books near an empty fireplace. He grabs one. "Here, Cassidy," he says. "What's the title of this book?"

I shrug.

"World War Two," I say, reading the red letters.

"Correct." He sits down on the coffee table, so I join Chris on the sofa. Walter flips through a few pages and adjusts his glasses. "Ah. Now what's this, Cassidy?"

I peer at the book, straining to make out the black and white images in the candlelight: candid shots of Japanese-Americans staring at the camera behind a wire fence.

"Internment camps," I say, looking up.

"Yes." Walter gets up and walks to another bookshelf. "During the 1940s, Japanese Americans were imprisoned in internment camps during the war. In Germany, Hitler sent millions of Germans and

Jews alike to concentration camps where they were either worked to death or executed in the gas chambers." He stops to take a slow breath. "Around the world, periodically, the populace is overtaken by a superior power and either enslaved, killed or freed. What we have in Omega is a force that is doing the first two as fast as they can."

I nervously wrap my hair around my finger.

"Why? Where did they come from? What country do they represent?" I say slowly.

"No country," Walter shrugs. "You look around town and you'll see posters advertising their presence." I take the poster I peeled off the wall out of my pocket and smooth it over my knee. He's right. "They represent not one country, but all," he goes on. "They seem to be some sort of emergency response force at first glance, but then again, their soldiers range in nationality from American to Russian. I've never seen anything like it."

"So who do they answer to?" I ask. "The U.S? The U.N.? South America? Who?"

"I couldn't say," Walter replies. "It's possible that they're some kind of branch of the United Nations...but that would come as a surprise to me. I've never seen an insignia like theirs before." He reaches out and studies the poster that's sitting in my lap. The O in Omega is four times as big as the rest of the letters, and once again, I'm left to look at all the continents of the earth that are crammed inside the O.

"So we don't know where they're from," I say. "What's they're purpose?"

"Who gives a damn?" Chris spits. "They're killing innocent people. Where's *our* military?"

"I heard rumors that our men were engaged in combat on the East Coast," Walter admits. "This *does* appear to be an invasion at first glance. Then again, all I know is what I see."

"How big is Omega? Do we know?"

"Does it matter?" Walter answers, taking his glasses off to wipe them on his shirt. "They are here, and that's what is important. They are killing us. I don't need to know why they're doing it – just that they *are*."

"Why aren't we *fighting* them? Is anybody even *trying*?" Chris demands. This time his anger is boiling, visible.

"I'm sure someone is trying, boy," Walter says. "But at the moment our country is very weak, isn't it? We were just struck with an EMP. Everyone's panicking. Our own government is completely dissolved without a way to communicate with its people. It has little to no power right now. What can they do to protect us? I'm sure there are military forces on the front lines, but they can't be everywhere at once. We were taken by surprise."

Chris leans forward.

"Sounds like Omega was ready to roll in before the EMP hit," he states. "Something like this takes planning. We saw more executions about forty miles from here. You think Omega's responsible for the EMP?"

"We may never know who *exactly* was behind the EMP," Walter replies. "And if I were you, I wouldn't dedicate your time to figuring out *why* or *how*. I would worry about staying alive *now*."

"But shouldn't we at least know *who's* trying to kill us?" I point out.

"No." Walter narrows his gaze. "Your life has one purpose, now. And that is to stay alive."

"You were in the military," Chris says suddenly.

"Yes," Walter sighs, setting the book down abruptly. "I was a pilot...a long time ago."

"During World War Two," I surmise.

"I was a history teacher for thirty years," he sighs. "I thought I'd seen it all, too. But this...*this* is a takeover. They're killing off anyone they think might get in their way. I saw this once. I never thought I'd see it here. And who knows how far it's spread?"

I stare at my coffee, sick.

"You saw this before in Germany," I say, bringing my eyes up to his. "The concentration camps. The Nazis."

He says nothing.

"I'm only alive right now because I wasn't stupid enough to run into the streets when everything went to hell," he replies, standing up again. "But I'll run out of food eventually. Not that I'm upset about that. I'm old enough to die, don't you think?"

I raise an eyebrow.

Walter rubs his hands on his pants again. A nervous habit?

"Do you live here alone?" Chris asks, his voice low.

"Now I do." Walter paces in front of the covered window. "They took my wife. First day. She went downstairs...haven't seen her since."

My throat seizes up.

"I'm so sorry," I say.

"It was her decision, not mine," he answers, but his voice is shaky.

"Thank you for letting us stay here," I tell him.

"You're not staying here," he corrects, turning around. His eyes are bright with tears. My heart breaks. "I brought you here so you wouldn't be shot for violating curfew. If you try to get out by just walking through the town at this point, you're dead. They've got guards posted on every block that leads out of the city."

"We got into the city fine," I point out.

"They're not trying to stop people from coming *in*," Walter says, picking up the coffeepot. Pouring a cup. "They're keeping people from going *out*."

Chris rests his arm against the back of the sofa.

"What are you saying, old man?"

Walter breaks into a wide smile.

"I know a safe way out of the city."

"And?"

"And to be honest, I just wanted to see if somebody could really pull it off."

Chris stands up, drinking the entire contents of the coffee cup in one gulp.

"Details?" he asks.

"There are tunnels under the city," Walter explains. "My wife..." he clears his throat, "was an architect. She helped build them. They were abandoned about fifteen years ago. I know how to get in, and all you have to do is follow them until you come to the end, which is well outside the city limits."

"Are you serious?" I exclaim. "Tunnels under the city?"

"All cities have secrets," Walter shrugs.

"How do we get to these tunnels?" Chris asks, not nearly as impressed as me.

"I'll show you," Walter says, "but we can't do it until it gets dark. It's too easy to be caught otherwise."

"Why haven't you gotten out of the city through the tunnels?" I demand. Is this a trap? "If they're such a good escape route, why are you still here?"

"Sweetheart, I'm eighty-seven years old," he replies, chuckling. "I'm not in any condition to be making a daring escape."

"Ah. Right," I cough.

"Are you hungry?" Walter asks.

"Starved," I reply.

"I'll get some food for you."

"We can't take your food," Chris says, being uncharacteristically kind to our host.

"Boy, I'm dying either way," he laughs. "No use worrying about me."

I sigh. What an optimist.

Chapter Eight

If there's one thing I know, it's that the United States of America has generally been a decent place to live. I mean, sure, it's not perfect by any stretch, but at least I have the freedom to walk down the street without getting shot.

It's safe. It's *home.*

Is it gone forever?

Chris and I take turns sleeping on the sofa in Walter's apartment. Regardless of whether or not we trust Walter, it's always wise for someone to keep watch. Resting in a warm room was something I sorely needed, and by the time nightfall, I feel energized.

Walter is pacing again.

"What's eating you, old man?" Chris asks, stretching his tall, lean frame over the couch. "You're not the one who's going to escape."

"But you're more than welcome to come with us," I add, shooting Chris a *look.*

Walter shakes his head.

"No, no," he says. "There's nothing in it for me. This better work, though."

He pulls out a thin sheet of white, virtually transparent paper. He shoves magazines and books off the coffee table and brings some of the candles closer. "What is it?" I ask, spreading the paper out.

"The tunnels," he says. "These plans belonged to my wife. The whole construction was meant to be a sort of a drainage system that would dump into a basin outside the city. Never did work right." His eyes mist over. "As far as I know, they're completely empty."

"Are you *sure*?" I press.

"I said as far as I know." He traces his finger along the route that we should take. Chris listens intently, studying the map from every angle.

How are we supposed to know what direction we're headed when we're traveling underground, anyway? What good does a map do when we'll have no light to read it with?

"What about light?" I ask. "Do you have any flashlights?"

"Sorry, no," Walter says. "Mine were electric. Dead."

"So we're going to go underground in the dark," I state. "We're going to die."

"We'll be fine," Chris replies. "You're not claustrophobic, though, are you?"

I run my fingers through my hair.

"Who isn't?" I grumble.

Chris pats me on the back, capturing one of my curly locks of hair around his finger. "Don't worry. I'll be there to keep you company." He smiles devilishly, standing close.

Closer than usual.

"Stop teasing," I say, flushing. "This is serious."

"I know." Chris looks at the map one more time. "It looks easy enough. We just follow the tunnel until it drops off at the basin."

"That's all there is to it," Walter nods. "It's a piece of cake."

"Get your stuff, Cassidy," Chris says. "It's time."

I stand from my cross-legged position on the floor and check my pack. I shrug my jacket on, twist my hair into a messy bun, and pull my boots back on.

"Ready," I say. "Ta-da."

Chris rolls of the couch and grabs his gear, pausing only to flick a non-existent piece of dust off the collar of my coat. His hand brushes my neck as he passes me. The touch is light. But to me, it ignites a firestorm of emotions in the pit of my stomach.

I scowl.

The flirting has *got* to stop.

Doesn't it?

I shake myself. I can't think about *that* right now. It's escape time.

Walter puts on an old wool jacket and pulls a crochet beanie over his head. A beanie that was made by his wife, no doubt.

Walter turns to us, smiling.

"Let's go, shall we?"

Chris squeezes my shoulders.

"Stick close," he whispers.

"Do as I do," Walter warns, opening the apartment door. I suddenly feel anxious, seeing the dark hallway.

Are we going to survive this?

Chris nudges me out the door, taking my hand in his. I exhale, charged with energy from that one simple gesture.

I could get used to life-threatening situations.

Walter locks the apartment door behind us, walking down the stairs. He's incredibly spry for an eighty-seven year-old man. When we reach the bottom level, he takes a long time opening the door and security bars. He exits first. Chris pauses at the door, waiting for the go-ahead.

"It's safe," Walter whispers.

Chris and I walk outside. It's dark. No floodlights, no guards as far as I can see. There *is* light in the distance, though, probably coming from the relief camps on the other side of the city.

Walter ducks into an alleyway.

"It's about a quarter of a mile from here," he whispers.

"What is?" I ask.

"Weren't you paying attention to everything we said inside?"

"No. It made no sense."

Chris releases a deep, soft laugh beside me.

"We're looking for the entrance to the tunnels," he explains.

"What does it look like?"

"You'll *see*," Walter stresses, obviously irritated that I didn't pay attention to his tunnel strategy/lecture upstairs.

Sorry, teacher. I zoned out.

We take several left and right-hand turns, Walter avoiding lighted areas. He stops at the corner of an abandoned Starbucks.

"There's a guard at the end of this block," he says.

I peek around the corner, spotting a blue-uniformed trooper ambling across the street with a flashlight. He sweeps the area and takes off to another part of the city.

"What's he looking for?" I wonder.

"Escapees," Walter says.

I swallow a huge lump in my throat. Walter moves across the street, leaving Starbucks behind. We approach the sidewalk. Walter points to a metal grate in the gutter.

"A gutter?" I say, deadpan. "How am I supposed to fit in *there*?"

"It's a lot bigger than it looks," he replies. "Trust me."

Chris kneels down and wraps his fingers around the grate, popping it out. Impressive.

Chris bends down.

"It *is* a lot bigger than it looks," he confirms. "Down you go."

"What? No. You go first."

He folds his arms. "You're scared."

"Um, *yeah*. It's a dark hole in the ground. Scary."

Chris stands up, enjoying this.

"Well, you can take it from here," Walter says.

We immediately turn our attention back to the old man with the crochet cap on his head.

"Thank you for your help," Chris says, shaking his hand, patting him on the back. "Are you sure you don't want to come with us?"

"This is my home," Walter replies. "I intend to keep it that way."

Walter looks at me.

"You keep an eye on him, okay?" he smiles.

"Whatever you say." I stand there fiddling with my jacket buttons, overcome with the urge to hug him. So I do. I throw my arms around his neck and pull him into a warm embrace.

"Everything will be okay," I say. "This isn't Nazi Germany. Not yet."

I step back.

"I believe you," he replies, taking my hand. "Be careful, both of you. And good luck."

Chris drops to his knees and slides under the metal plating of the gutter. He rolls over the side of the cement slope and disappears into the hole. I freeze, waiting for him to hit the bottom.

I hear a soft thud, then, "Your turn, Cassie."

I turn around and kiss Walter on the cheek.

"Thank you," I say.

I get down on my hands and knees and crawl under the sidewalk. The cement slopes downward, covered with wet leaves. I swallow and whisper, "Here I come."

I roll off the slope, twisting to brace for the impact. I land on my feet, halfway on the ground, halfway on top of Chris. He catches me, softening the landing.

"Good thing you don't weigh much," he grunts.

It's impossible to see down here. A thin stream of light is coming from the gutter opening above our heads. It's almost completely extinguished as Walter puts the gutter grill back on, propping it against the sidewalk.

"I've never heard of a gutter this size," I say. "This is against so many safety regulations."

"That's the least of our problems." Chris reaches for my hand and holds on tight. "Don't let go. Just trust that I know where I'm going."

"I don't," I reply, "but I still won't let go."

I reach out to touch the wall. My fingers brush something wet and slimy. I stifle a girlish squeal and wipe my hands on my pants. My shoes sink ankle-deep into cold, smelly sludge.

"No talking unless absolutely necessary," Chris says.

"What if somebody else is down here? Somebody bad?" I ask.

"The chances of that are slim. Come on."

"You didn't answer my question."

"Because I didn't want to." A few beats of infuriating silence go by before he continues. "If there is someone down here, that would make it even more important to be quiet. Yes?"

I nod.

"Cassidy?"

"I nodded! We're not supposed to talk, remember?"

He laughs quietly and we keep moving. I have to bend down to avoid hitting my head on the low ceiling.

"I thought these tunnels were supposed to be empty," I say, water and sludge slapping the walls.

"They're abandoned," Chris whispers, "not empty. Relax. Walking through raw sewage is better than being arrested."

Sewage?

This day just keeps getting better.

Because Chris is so much taller than me, he has to bend down farther to avoid hitting his head on the roof of the tunnel.

After several minutes I ask,

"How much farther?"

"About a mile."

"A *mile*!?"

"Shhh." Chris slaps his hand over my mouth. "Quiet, remember?"

I move his hand away from my face, noting just how stale and pungent the air is down here. I had expected a cold, freezing tunnel system. Instead it's almost warm, as if no air ever enters the tunnels.

Periodically we hear odd dripping noises or the distant pattering of small feet. Rats? Bugs? I press my lips together. I don't want to inhale any insects. I've seen one too many horror movies to do that.

If Chris is perturbed about being stuck in a hole in the ground, I don't sense it. His body is relaxed, loose. His breathing is even.

"This is suffocating..." I begin, trailing off as the sound of an engine cuts through the tunnels. It begins as a soft sound, escalating to a full roar. I clap my hands over my ears. The tunnel feels like it's shaking. Above us, a faint stream of light is painted across the concrete wall. The tunnel opens up into a wide space under the sidewalk. Another entrance.

"We must be close to the city center," Chris says into my ear. "That's another gutter opening."

"What's that noise?"

"Trucks."

He feels for my hand again. For a few seconds, I can see his face outlined in the shadows cast by the light of the streets above. I breathe in the current of cold air flowing through the opening, freezing. A voice cuts through the silence:

"Take that one to the camp. I'll take care of things here."

A door slams. Another engine starts. Shadows flit across the light pouring in from the street. Chris tenses up slightly and tugs on my hands. "Move."

I get to my feet. We hunker back down and slip into the continuation of the tunnel. The light disappears again, and this time the water is up to my calves. It's also getting colder, the farther we progress. A change from the stale temperatures we ran into before.

I take the opportunity to think about everything Walter told us in the apartment about Omega and wonder why nobody has ever heard of them before. How could we be invaded by an army that has no country, no king, and most importantly – how could no one even know that these people existed? Why do the troops speak different languages? Are they *all* paid hit men, and if so, where did

99

Omega find enough people to create an army big enough to invade an entire country? How long have they been planning this?

A very long time, my inner voice whispers.

Every once in a while we come to another gutter opening, tiptoe past the lights and voices, and slip into the next tunnel. It's impossible to get lost. There is only *one* tunnel. We keep going until our necks ache from being continually hunched over. Until the smell of rotting leaves is permanently stamped into our brains.

"Smell that?" Chris suddenly says.

"What?"

"Fresh air."

I sniff, catching a whiff of cold, clean air.

"We must be at the basin," I say.

"Yeah. That was faster than I thought."

Sure. Only two solid hours of tromping through the sewers.

Piece of cake.

We pick up the pace, following the clean scent of open air. Chris stops unexpectedly and we bump into a solid wall. I experience a flash of panic. Is it a dead-end?

Please don't this be a dead-end.

"Huh," Chris murmurs, sliding his palm across the cement. "Ah."

"What is it?"

"The tunnel's curving." He walks forward and sure enough, we both follow the wall into a neat left hand turn.

I clap my hands together, natural light spilling into the tunnel. Even though it's nighttime, it seems extraordinarily bright compared to the total blackness of being underground.

"Freedom!" I exclaim.

I jog forward, getting down and crawling on my hands and knees toward the exit. Chris crawls behind me. Spatters of rain blow across my face. I come to the edge of the tunnel, cautiously observing the environment. I inch forward, peeking outside. The first thing I see is an expanse of darkness. It must be the empty basin. The second thing I see is the sky. The third thing I see is Chris crouching in the mouth of the tunnel, a frown on his face.

Because then my *other* senses kick in and I *hear* it: water lapping against the side of the basin. I squint at it again, my eyes adjusting to the light.

The basin is full of water.

"What?!" I exclaim, shocked. "He said this thing was *empty*! Where did all this water come from?"

"Not from this tunnel, obviously." Chris is rubbing his chin. "It's about twenty feet from here to the top of the basin. It's a slope. You can climb it."

"How deep do you think that water is?" I ask, sticking my hand out. I dip my finger into the water. It leaves traces of silt on my fingertips.

"Doesn't matter," Chris shrugs. "The only thing that matters is that we're out of the city, and we did it without getting arrested."

I take a deep breath.

I stand up and wrap my hands around the top of the tunnel, leaning over the water and looking up. Chris is right. The top of the basin is only about twenty feet away, and it's sloped enough that we can scale it.

"Go ahead," I say, shivering.

"Ladies always go first," Chris replies, standing up beside me. "I'll be right behind you."

I grimace, swinging my feet out of the tunnel and into the hard surface of the basin. The sound of the water lapping against the dirt is disturbing to me, because if there's one thing I hate even more than small, dark spaces, it's dark, dirty water.

I dig my hands into the dirt and lie on my stomach against the ground. The angle's not too bad. I climb on my hands and knees, hearing a soft *pat* as Chris swings onto the ground below me.

"Race you to the top," I say.

"Get ready to lose, kid," he grins.

I pick up the speed. I start laughing, enjoying myself for the first time since...well, since the apocalypse.

"Eat my dust," I tease, turning my head up toward the top of the basin.

I inhale sharply. We've got company.

A tall, thin man is casually observing our progress.

I lose my footing on the dirt and begin sliding backwards. The guy is standing motionless, watching us, making no move to do anything violent. Chris grabs my legs as I slide down, pushing me back up. "Careful..." he whispers, his eyes trained on the guy.

"What do you want?" he asks.

The guy cocks his head to the side and brushes his coat behind his hips. Even against the night sky I can see the gleam of his teeth from his smile.

"Chris..." I murmur, worried.

"You popped up on the wrong side of town," he says.

"What's it to you?" Chris asks, and in my opinion, he is *far* more intimidating than anyone we've come across yet.

"Nothing. Just making a comment, man."

Chris urges me to keep climbing. I hesitate. Every inch puts me closer to the stranger. "What you got in those packs?" the guy asks. "Any food? Water?"

"Nothing that belongs to you," I say.

The guy laughs.

"Maybe it *does*."

I climb to the right, coming up on the other side of the guy. He still doesn't move, even as I climb to my feet and stand at the top of the basin. Chris draws himself up to his full height and steps in front of me.

"Move on," he warns. "Now."

The guy has wide, bloodshot eyes. Now that I'm standing a few feet away from him, I can see the obvious tears and blood on his shirt. He's hurt, and by the looks of it, starving.

"Maybe we should..." I start to say.

Chris cuts me off, indicating that I should start walking away. I look around the basin. There is a chain link fence surrounding the property, but thanks to a stroke of luck, there's no barbed wire.

"Just give me the packs, man," the guy says, and this time his voice has a note of warning. "Come on. Help a guy out."

Chris holds his hands up and takes a few steps backwards, pushing me with him. "Not today. Sorry."

"Not as sorry as you're going to be."

The man moves lightening-quick. For somebody who looks like he's bleeding to death, he sure doesn't act like it. He strikes out at

Chris's face with nothing but his fist. Chris blocks the blow with hardly any effort, snapping the guy's arm back and kicking him to the ground.

The guy isn't done yet, though. He springs back to his feet and flings off his jacket, revealing toned, muscular arms. "You wanna fight? I can do that," he growls, wiping his nose. "Come on."

"Your funeral," Chris says under his breath.

I roll my eyes, watching the testosterone-fueled gladiator match play out before my eyes.

Chris ducks his head, avoiding a right hook. They circle each other for a few seconds. Chris prowls around him like a cat, twice as tall and far more knowledgeable in self-defense than this street fighter.

Maybe the guy realizes that Chris is going to pound him into a pulp, or maybe he really *is* as wounded as he looks – because he turns around, looks right at me, and rips the pack off my back. He grabs my arms and whips around the other side of me, literally flinging me to the ground. I hit the dirt on my shoulder, tumbling tail over teakettle down the edge of the basin. I roll all the way to the bottom, scraping my face up in the process.

I hear yelling and scuffling in the background, but all of that disappears when I plunge sideways into the cold water of the basin. The shock of the freezing water is jarring. Horrible. I can't even move, completely submerged in black water. I can't see anything. I can't even feel the walls of the basin. Then my instincts flare and I begin kicking upward, breaking the surface, sputtering for air. I'm only around eight feet away from the bank, so I start swimming toward it, hating that I have no idea how deep the water is – or what's *in* it.

Above me, the guy is laid out on the ground. Chris tosses him down the bank, starting a long tumble.

What is this? Public swimming appreciation day?

Chris slides down after him, upright, keeping his balance perfectly. The guy skids to a halt right before the water, about two feet away from me. He reaches out and dunks my head under the water – just to spite me, I guess. Nice.

The next thing I know, his hand is gone, I'm breaking the surface again, and the guy is about ten feet away in the water, having been thrown there by Chris.

Chris grabs me by the belt of my pants and pulls me onto the dirt. He's got a bloody lip, but other than that, he looks great.

As always.

I shiver, disliking the feel of my wet clothes against the soil.

"Now what?" I ask, coughing up water. Chris links his arms under my shoulders, pulls me to my feet. "Are you just going to leave him there?"

"Maybe it'll teach him a lesson," he says, combing my hair back from my face. "Are you okay?"

"I'm fine," I nod. "Just wet."

Chris helps me climb up the side of the basin again while the guy kicks and flails around in the water, not bothering to give chase. I guess getting your butt handed to you by a Navy SEAL has a way of killing your motivation.

Chris picks up my backpack from the ground and swings it around his shoulder. "I can carry that," I say, my teeth chattering.

"I got it," he replies. "Take your coat off and try to get it dry."

I peel off the fabric, feeling my skin tighten as the cold wind hits. Chris casts a final glance at the guy, who's pulling himself out of the water and crawling to the other side of the basin.

"Punk," he mutters.

"Maybe all he wanted was a little help."

Chris places his hand on the small of my back, motioning for us to move.

"He didn't ask *politely*."

"He was desperate."

"He was rude." He touches my waist. "I don't tolerate rude."

We come to the chain-link fence. Chris climbs it without any trouble. I manage to scramble over the top. The two of us continue walking back toward the highway. It's clearly visible from here. In fact, it's impossible to miss.

"Do you think Walter will be okay?" I ask quietly.

"Yes." Chris steps over a broken scooter. How the heck did a *scooter* get out in the middle of a grassy field? "Don't worry about him, Cassidy. We have our own problems."

"There's really no place left that's safe, is there? They've probably taken over every city." I pause. "And who is *they* anyway? What does Omega really want? How is it possible that somebody we've never heard of has started setting up death camps all over the flipping state?"

"Good question." Chris thinks it over for a second. "It would make sense that they're a U.N.-based group. Where else would they come from? How else would they be ready for this? But it's amazing to me that nobody's doing anything to stop it."

"Maybe they can't," I reply, frowning. "The EMP disabled all of our technology, right? Maybe our military is suffering just as much as we are. Hey, you don't think...?" I trail off.

Chris casts a sideways glance at me.

"What?" he asks.

"You don't think this whole EMP thing was an inside job?" I say. "Maybe whoever is behind Omega planned it and then they were just waiting to roll in and take over. Does that make any sense?"

"It makes perfect sense," Chris replies. "The question is, *who* is orchestrating it?"

"And why?" I add. "Man, this sucks."

Understatement of the century.

Chris claps me on the shoulder.

"No, it could be worse," he assures me. "And we're going to be fine."

"Considering it's the end of the world, I don't know if *fine* is the word I would use to describe our situation."

"We're better off than most people," Chris smiles. I mean, *really* smiles. It's gorgeous. No doubt about it. Because he's not wearing a jacket, his shirt is soaking from the constant drizzle, sticking to his muscles in all the right places.

"You're staring at me," he states, snapping me out of my reverie.

"I am *not*," I laugh nervously. "I'm just...thinking. Without blinking."

Chris breaks into good-natured laughter.

"Sure you are."

I roll my eyes, feigning innocence. He doesn't need to know how I feel. It would go to his head. Instantly.

"What about food and water?" I ask, trying to change the subject. "We're going to run out."

"We'll figure something out," Chris says.

"How can you be so *calm* about starving? And dehydration? You know how long it's been since I've peed?"

I could have left that last part out, I guess.

To my surprise, Chris doesn't take the opportunity to tease me. Instead he says, "Drink what water you have left in your canteen. We'll stop for the night and as long as it rains you can keep drinking. Dehydration is more deadly than going without food for a couple of days, so we'll address that problem first. We can use the poncho in your backpack to gather more water if you want."

"Great. I'm going to die."

"Don't be dramatic," says.

"I'm not being dramatic. I'm being realistic."

Chris shoots me an annoyed look, but doesn't say anything. After we get around five miles out of Bakersfield, I'm still wet. Still tired. We find an old truck with a camper shell and crawl inside. A box of fishing gear is sitting in the trunk. I rummage through the contents.

"There's no river nearby, is there?" I ask as Chris shuts the door.

"He was driving northbound," he shrugs. "Probably headed to the mountains." He twirls a camping permit in his fingers. "Kings Canyon."

I open my pack and turn on the crank radio and electric lamp. Chris decides to be noble and wind the radio up while I get out "dinner," which is nothing more than another bland energy bar.

"Got anything?" I ask, peeling the wrapper back.

Chris sets the radio on the floor.

Silence.

"Looks like the days of the radio are over," Chris announces, a tinge of sadness in his voice. "What's for dinner?"

"Turkey and potatoes," I deadpan, tossing him a bar. "And for dessert, pumpkin pie."

"Someone's got Thanksgiving dinner on their mind," Chris says, amused. "What did you do last time?"

"For Thanksgiving?" I yawn. "I made dinner for me and my dad and then we watched *How the West Was Won*."

Chris laughs.

"Your mom must appreciate all your cooking."

I frown, tearing my energy bar into tiny little pieces.

"I wouldn't know."

Maybe he notices my mood change. Maybe he's just curious.

But he asks, "Where's your mother, Cassidy?"

I avoid his eyes, finding a loose thread on my jacket sleeve to focus on. "Not sure," I shrug. "Why?"

"Do you have any family besides your father?"

"Not really, no." I look up, uncomfortable. "And this is important to you *because*...?"

"I'm just asking," Chris says, throwing his hands up.

But I can tell there's more to it than that.

"Where are *your* parents?" I ask, raising my eyebrows.

Chris takes a bite of his bar, giving me a *look*.

"They're retired," he replies.

"Both of them?"

He nods.

"What did they do?"

"They were farmers," he says.

"What about your brother?"

"Senior in high school."

I smile mischievously.

"Is he cute?" I ask. "Or single?"

Chris stops chewing and leans forward.

"And this matters to you because...?" he echoes, raising an eyebrow.

"Just asking," I grin. "But seriously. Is your brother cute?"

"Not as cute as me." He winks.

He actually *winks*, and somehow it comes across as sexy rather than stupid. I feel myself blushing, and I am extremely grateful that it's so dark inside the camper shell.

"Well, you're not cute," I say, finishing off my bar.

"*I'm* not cute?" Chris repeats, looking shocked. "Is that why you stare at me all the time?"

"I'm not staring at you!" I retort. "I'm just making sure you're not trying to kill me. Or steal my backpack."

"Right. A backpack with bland energy bars and a plastic poncho." He smirks. "That's been my plan all along."

"Hey, desperation drives people to do crazy things," I say.

"You still don't think I'm cute?"

His smile is playful. Pleasant, even.

"No," I say, and it's the truth. Chris isn't *cute*. He's way too mature and fit and *older* to be cute. He's *hot*. But he doesn't need to know that's what I think.

"You're a terrible liar," he says, folding his arms across his chest. "You're smiling."

"I'm not smiling," I answer. "I'm laughing at *you*. Vanity is so yesterday."

"Ah." He suddenly reaches across the truck and places his arms right over my head. I freeze, surprised – and stunned.

"My brother," he says, his face *way* too close, "is very similar to me. But he's eleven years younger than I am."

I hold my breath, my eyes flicking down to the fine hair around his mouth, up the sides of his cheeks. He's got nice skin, a strong jaw, long, thick hair right above the shoulders. Dark brown with blonde highlights. A perfect combination.

"Chris," I whisper, afraid to breathe.

He moves closer. Way too close. I can actually feel him breathing against my skin, and he smells a little like the leftover coffee from Walter's apartment. His eyes search my face. His gaze is so intense that it would be a crime to move. To *blink*. And if I lean forward just an *inch*, I could kiss him.

I can almost feel his lips on mine. It's dizzying.

"What...time is it?" I ask, glancing down at the crank radio, dropping my eyes. I can see the time from here: 8:33 p.m.

He knows I can see it, too. But instead of pointing that out, he slowly moves his arms from the camper shell and pulls away, making a point of taking his time fingering the strands of hair falling over my shoulder. He doesn't appear to be angry. He's not thrilled, either.

That could be a good thing. Or a bad thing.

I finally exhale, daring to breathe once again. And I'm *hot* – burning up. What should I say? Something like: "Why didn't you kiss me?" or "Why did I ask for the *time*?"

Chris says nothing, retreating into frustrating silence. I curl up into my usual ball and try to say warm as Chris flicks off the light. I crack one of the windows open, tipping the mouth of my canteen toward the sky. Every drop makes a soft, relaxing sound. It soothes me. Cools me off.

Eventually I fall asleep, but it takes me a long time, because I'm hyperaware of Chris's body only a few feet away, and I *know* that he's watching my silhouette in the darkness. I can feel it.

It's the most exciting, puzzling thing I've ever experienced.

Well. Besides the end of the world.

At dawn, I sit up quickly because my feet are cold. Rainwater is dripping through the window, pooling over my boots. I groan and pull my legs backward.

Chris's arm is thrown across the truck bed like he owns it, the other arm behind his head. I study his face, finding myself smiling in the process. He looks relaxed, almost boyish in sleep. The hard lines of his face are much softer, less guarded.

I grab my canteen. It's full. The sky is still dark but it doesn't seem to be raining. Awesome.

Chris stretches and sits up, running a hand through his hair.

"It's not raining," is the first thing he says.

"Thank God."

Chris smiles. "I agree. Breakfast?"

I dig into my pack. There are three packages of energy bars left, which means we've got about fifteen bars left. I hand him one, shutting the window. After we're done with our gourmet breakfast, we exit the truck. It's colder than yesterday, a definite temperature change.

I button up my jacket, feeling bad for Chris because the only jacket he has is comprised of ruined leather. Not ideal.

"So," I say, staring down the road. "I guess we have a lot of walking to do."

Chris puts his arm around my shoulders, a grin lurking at the corners of his mouth. "Fear not, little maiden," he replies, "the road may be long, but the journey will be worth it."

I stare at him.

"Seriously? Is that a line from a movie?"

Chris gives me an exasperated look.

"You're impossible to impress," he says, shifting his backpack.

As we begin walking I ask, "So what kind of stuff do you have in *your* pack? Any food? Maybe some candy?"

"No food," Chris replies. "I was biking for the day in Santa Monica when the EMP hit. I was *planning* to go back to San Diego and eat dinner."

"So do you live on the military base?" I grin. "Do you get to drive in a convoy everywhere?"

Chris chuckles.

"No," he says. "I live in an apartment in Santee."

"Santee? Why?"

"I'm not active duty anymore, Cassidy. I can't live on a base." He looks sad for a second, but quickly hides the emotion on his face. "It's a beautiful city."

"It's *dry*," I remark.

"It's a desert by the sea." Chris opens his arms out wide. "And I don't think Culver City is any more lush with plant life than Santee."

"Culver City happens to be within ten minutes of Hollywood, Beverly Hills *and* Santa Monica," I point out. "I can visit the Walk of Fame on the weekends."

"Santee is thirty minutes away from the Pacific Ocean and the birthplace of California," Chris argues. "Not to mention some of the best surfing spots on the coast."

"You *surf?*" I ask, astonished.

"I'm a SEAL. I adapt to water." He glances at me. "What about you?"

"Oh, sure. I adapt to water about as much as a rock does."

He laughs.

"Not the aquatic type?" he teases. "I guess you don't exactly have a swimmer's build."

"What's *that* supposed to mean?" I cross my arms.

"Swimmers are generally tall, with long arms and legs."

"Nobody's ever heard of a petite swimmer before?"

"Stranger things have happened," he admits.

I mock-punch him in the arm.

"Don't make fun of my height," I warn. "I'm tiny but mighty."

"I don't doubt it." Chris reaches over and pinches my waist. "Sometime I'll show you how to surf."

"Awesome. Just you, me and the circling sharks." I give him a thumbs up. "Fun."

"It will be," he shrugs. "You'll make a perfect decoy."

"Meaning...?"

"You can distract the sharks while I surf."

"Brilliant military strategy, my friend. All those years of training finally paid off."

We both burst into laughter. Such an odd conversation. Yet somehow it's nice to be able to talk to someone and be completely ridiculous.

It makes it easier. All of this.

The day passes without incident. We have several conversations concerning conspiracy theories about the EMP and the murder of innocent civilians by the phantom military force calling itself Omega. Where did the EMP come from? Was it *from* Omega? Was it from somebody else? Maybe it's nothing more than a hoax, a massive joke that will cause a huge scandal a month from now.

Then I remember the bodies.

This is no joke.

In the process of discussing our many doomsday theories, I learn more about Chris. Where he's from. Who he is.

"I joined the military because I didn't have any money to go to college," he says.

We pass a decrepit green Honda.

Seventy-five, I think. *That's the seventy-fifth one I've seen today.*

"Becoming a SEAL wasn't something I planned on. I just wanted the training. I always liked beating people up, you know," he jokes, "so the combat aspect of it appealed to me."

"Unsurprising," I remark. "And you've traveled a lot, right?"

"Yeah." He takes a deep breath, as if the memory is painful. "My first tour was in Iraq. That lasted for three years. Then I came back to base for a couple of months and I got shipped out again. I went to Iraq three times, then Afghanistan twice. I've been everywhere."

"What did you do there?" I ask, impressed with his travel repertoire.

"Fight the bad guys," he states simply.

"So you were a SEAL for about nine years," I say. "That's pretty cool."

"Yeah, maybe."

"And where'd you get that tattoo on your arm?" I ask, referring to the cobra on his bicep. "That does *not* seem like something your mother would approve of."

Chris rubs his jaw.

"My mother...would understand."

"Oh, so she *doesn't* know?" I laugh. "Afraid to face the music?"

"You haven't met my mother."

"I'm pretty sure she can't compete with my mom's scariness."

"Want to bet?"

"You'll lose." I giggle. "And then I'll tell your mother."

"You're very funny, Cassidy," Chris says. "Ha. Ha."

"Yeah, I know," I reply. "So why'd your family move from Virginia to California?"

"My mother was from California," he explains. "She always wanted to move back. When I joined the military, they left Virginia and came here. Got a nice piece of a land up in the foothills, set way back from the road. My brother's in a charter school."

"I did a charter school," I say. "It wasn't really my thing."

"Yeah? Why not?"

"The classes were boring."

Chris smiles. It's a beautiful sight. He says something, but being preoccupied with my own thoughts, I ask him to repeat it.

"I said, *lucky you*," he repeats, entertained. "And you're staring at me again."

"I am *not.*"

"My smile must be dazzling."

"*Please.*" I wave him off. "You're so full of it."

"No. I just notice things."

He reaches out and touches my cheek – barely a feathery brush against my skin, but it sends a rush of heat from my face to the tips of my toes. I snap out of it and continue to walk, aware of his every movement. I steal a glance at his face, peeking through my hair. He's watching me, and as I turn away, he smiles.

This game of peek-a-boo is escalating quickly.

We stop and rest a few times, sitting beside the center freeway divider, discussing favorite television shows and musical artists. Chris is far more conservative than I am in that respect. I like my soap operas juicy. He doesn't like them at all. So I educate him on the wonders of dramatic television while he attempts to convince me of the merit of military reality shows.

Yeah. Probably not going to happen.

By the time it starts to get dark again, the rain clouds are breaking up just enough to let some blue sky through. It's nice to know that the world won't stay gray forever, even if World War III *is* upon us.

We make camp in another car again.

At around nine o'clock, I crank the radio and tune into every available station. Nothing. Are they dead? With my knowledge of Omega's presence here, I wonder...have the stations really died? Maybe they've just been *commandeered.*

God. What better way to lure people into concentration camps than to call them "emergency relief camps" and then broadcast the message to every radio in the state? It's freaking genius.

I hate you, I think bitterly. *Whoever you are, I hope somebody finds you and takes you down.*

I try to relax afterward. I don't want to think about my dad. I might start believing that he never made it out of L.A. I don't want to think about my mom working at the hotel in Culver City. I pray she made it out alive, too. I didn't have many friends back home, so besides my estranged mom and maybe-alive father, I don't have many people to worry about.

Story of my life.

At ten, I drop off to sleep. I don't dream about anything, but at midnight I wake up gasping for breath. My heart is racing. My headache has returned. I'm also covered in cold sweat. Disturbed, I prop myself up against the inside of the car and get comfortable. It doesn't help. I feel sick. Maybe I *am* sick. Days of traveling on foot, with little food, barely enough water and more than enough traumatic experiences to last a lifetime?

Yeah. I might have caught something.

That's when I hear the voices. They're close. I freeze like a deer in headlights, forgetting my discomfort.

Male voices...I *think*. Several. A yellow beam of light flashes through the air and I drop to my stomach. Somebody is walking down the interstate. Granted, they could be survivors like Chris and me, but they could also be thugs. Like crowbar boy back in Santa Clarita.

"Chris," I whisper, tugging on his sleeve. "Hello. Wake *up!*"

He snaps awake. I grab his arm and force his head down. "There are *people* outside," I hiss.

Chris knits his brow, making a move to grab his gun and whatever weapon he's been keeping hidden in his pant pocket. My fingernails are digging into his skin because I'm gripping his arm so hard. "Sorry," I whisper.

He pats my cheek. Under normal circumstances I would have blushed, but another flashlight beam slides across the road. Then two more. I peek my head over the bottom of the window, spotting three figures in the darkness. They're tall, masculine and they've got *rifles* slung across their backs.

"Big. Strong. Armed," I breathe, sufficiently spooked. "If they find us, we're toast."

"We don't know they're our enemies yet. But until we do we can assume that they are," Chris whispers. He makes sure his gun is loaded. He hands me a heavy Bowie knife. "Use this if you have to."

I nod.

"But you can feel free to go ahead and shoot them first," I advise. "Knives aren't my forte. I almost cut off my thumb once when I was slicing a tomato."

"Really, Cassie?" He says, a tremor of laughter in his voice. "Focus."

"Right. Sorry."

Just then, the strangers' flashlights go out. I will myself to remain motionless, to stop breathing.

Be a statue, I tell myself.

It's dark, and their voices vanish altogether. Chris tenses beside me, his hand on my shoulder. Neither of us is willing to speak and give ourselves away.

Drip drop.

Rain?

I scream. The trunk of the SUV pops open and three powerful flashlights are shined directly in our faces, blinding us. Chris throws his arm in front of me, pushing me backwards, and holds his gun up defensively.

At first, the light is so glaring that I can't begin to see the faces of the people who are holding them. But I *can* hear their voices.

"Well," someone says. Young male voice. "What have we got here?"

His face comes into view. He's tall, short black hair cut to the scalp. Pinched face. The guy next to him is around the same age, same haircut. The last guy is younger than the rest, but stocky. Probably powerful.

The second two are also pointing their rifles at us.

Chris doesn't lower his weapon, and for a few *really* long seconds everyone trades glances with each other like we're stuck on the *pause* mode of a DVD player.

"Put down the weapon, man," the main guy says. The one with the black hair. "We'll blow your head off if you try to shoot us."

Chris, realizing that we're literally backed into a hole, slowly lowers his gun and sets it on the floor. Guy Number Two grabs the gun and stuffs it into his belt, grinning.

"Pretty girl," he says, looking right at me. "*Real* pretty. Remember me?"

If there were such a thing as a literal death stare, Chris would have killed all three of them with the intense glare he's shooting their way. I simply blink a couple of times. Because the guy I'm looking at is the same jerk that pushed me into the basin in Bakersfield. I can even see the bruises on his face where Chris beat the crap out of him.

Has he been *tracking* us?

"What do you want?" Chris asks.

His voice is a lot calmer than his body language.

"Just sniffing out rats, man," Main Dude replies. "We found a couple. Climb on outta there. You too, baby." He holds his hand out to me. I ignore the gesture and step onto the pavement, Chris right beside me. "That's right. Nice and easy."

Main Dude looks me over, a sick smirk crawling across his face.

"Not bad. Not bad at all." He motions to the backpack. "Got anything *this* time?"

"No," I lie.

Guy Number Two shoves the cold barrel of his rifle into my back.

"Don't lie to us," he warns.

"I'm not. There's nothing in there but...feminine products." I bite my lip. "You can have them if you want, but I can't see why a couple of macho guys like you would be interested. I mean, that's just *wrong.*"

Main Dude's mouth twitches. He flicks his finger underneath my chin, inspecting my face. "She always like this?" he asks, looking at Chris.

He shrugs.

Main Dude smiles. It's not a comforting smile. It's gross.

He says, "I think we can use you." He turns to Chris. "You, on the other hand, I can't think of a reason to keep alive."

"Whoa!" I say. "What do you want? Supplies? Just take them and *go*. You don't have to do this."

"We're just staying off the radar, baby," Main Dude says. "And enjoying it while we do."

"Staying off the radar?" I repeat. "Meaning Omega's radar, right?"

"They're everywhere, man." He shakes his head. "Like roaches."

"So let us go," I say. "We're just trying to do the same thing."

"Yeah, but you're a pretty girl, and I wouldn't mind your company back at camp," he replies. "Come on."

He grabs me around the waist and pulls me forward. Scared, I don't think about what I do. But I do it. I bring the tip of my elbow up and jam it into his mouth. Hard. He stumbles backwards, bewildered, right as Chris literally *rips* the rifle out of Guy Number Two's hands and smashes the butt against his head.

Guy Number Two hits the ground, out cold – maybe dead – when I spin around, face to face with Guy Number Three. He grabs me by the hair and jams the heavy side of *his* gun into my stomach, knocking the air out of my lungs.

Gee, thanks for *that*.

I almost puke as I stumble backwards and hit the car, landing on my butt on the pavement. Three moves toward me, only to be put in a headlock by Chris, who slams his head against the car. He passes out, too. Which leaves Mr. Main Dude. But instead of standing like a man and fighting, he takes off into the night, running, screaming, "Over here! Come on!"

Chris bends down and hoists me up with one sweep of his arm.

122

"You all right?" he asks, only slightly winded. Like beating up a couple of guys is just a walk in the park. "Cassidy?"

I shake myself, my headache pounding worse than ever. "Fine," I murmur. "He's going for backup, you know."

"I know." Chris doesn't let go of my hand as he rounds the car, grabbing our backpacks. He hands me mine and helps me put it on. Then he bends down and grabs his gun from Guy Number Two's belt, also shouldering the shotguns from both unconscious cronies. "You take one," he says.

"Are you kidding? I can't shoot that thing."

Chris slings both of them across his back.

"Fine. Let's hustle before he comes back."

Chris pulls me along, tossing me one of their flashlights. I catch it. It almost slips through my sweaty fingers. Chris and I jog for a long time before we slow to a more even pace.

"Wait," I say. "Slow down."

"We have to keep going," Chris replies, "I'd rather not deal with an entire gang – although I will if I have to."

"I just want to get some pain meds," I plead, trying to find the medicine box in the dark. "My head hurts."

"Still?" Chris's voice sounds concerned. "Why didn't you tell me?"

"People get headaches, Chris. It's not like I got shot."

I wince with the pain of the migraine, unable to tell if I'm sweating from a fever or from running for half an hour. I flick the flashlight on as I dig around, finally closing in on the pain meds. I chew several up, much to Chris's disapproval.

"That's too many," he says, looking frustrated. "Don't overdose."

"It's *children's* medication."

I zip the pack up and get to my feet. Shaky, sweaty, migraine-ridden. All in all, considering that it's the end of the world, I'm in pretty good shape.

Right?

Chapter Nine

Twenty-four hours later, it's one o'clock in the morning and foggy. *Very* foggy. There's no more than five-foot visibility. I keep close to Chris as we follow the road, listening for suspicious sounds and watching for lights. My headache remains, but it's not pounding like it was. I can thank the pain meds for that.

Glad I had them in my go-bag.

We haven't seen any sign of Main Dude or a comeback posse. Good thing, too. There's a strong possibility that Chris would simply shoot them all if they showed up. It's a relief. I'd like to survive this experience without my travel partner going total ninja warrior on me.

We eventually stop and kick back on the side of the road, deciding that no one will be able to sneak up on us because nobody can *see* us through the fog. I throw my hood over my head because the fog is heavy – like a blanket pressing down on my skin. It simulates the feeling of suffocation. Imagine inhaling thick, hot steam for hours on end. Only *this* steam isn't hot. It's cold, but equally as penetrating.

When my headache begins to return – and the fever – I take more medication to keep the severity of the pain away. I don't feel great, but at least I'm not dying. Chris doses off for a little while and I do the same, slumping next to him with my head on his shoulder.

We start moving at three-thirty, having covered at least another fifteen miles since last night. "I should have been a cross-country marathon runner," I say.

I wish we could stop at a restaurant. Eat junk food.

Oh, man. Junk food.

I miss you…

"You're doing very well," Chris assures me. "Taking it like a soldier."

"Thanks," I say, uninspired.

We stop again at six o'clock, just as the sun is coming up. Only we can't really see the sun through all the fog, so the scenery turns from black to gray. At seven we pick up the pace and I spot a McDonald's off the freeway.

"Chris," I say. "I need more food than an energy bar to stay alive. Can we at least *peek* inside one of the restaurants along the freeway? There might be something inside that we can eat."

"Cassidy, that's highly unlikely," Chris replies. "Besides, we need to stay on the road and out of the cities."

"This isn't a *city*," I point out. "This is the middle of nowhere. The only residents are coyotes and rats."

Chris sighs, but he doesn't argue. We're both starving, and the lack of calories is beginning to take its toll on our bodies – especially mine. It's been six days since we've had anything besides the allotted protein bar.

I climb over the center divider, cutting across the freeway exit ramp toward a McDonald's. There are no cars in the parking lot – or at the gas station across the street. A more positive sign is that the windows haven't been smashed out of the McDonald's yet.

Hooray.

I jog toward it. Posters of hamburgers and milkshakes are glued to the windows. Nothing could be better right now. Or *sound* better, anyway. I walk up to the front door and push. It doesn't budge.

Chris tugs on the handle and walks around the building, checking the entries and exit points. Finally he says, "We'll have to break in."

"Awesome," I say. "I'll kick in the door."

"Thank you, but I think I'd better handle this part," Chris replies, smiling dryly. "Excuse me."

He pulls his Bowie knife out of my belt and slips it between the glass double doors. It's only a matter of seconds before he pops the lock.

"After you," Chris says, holding the door open.

I walk inside, impressed with his thief-like skills.

"You should have been a professional bank robber," I tell him.

"Yeah, my mother would have really loved that."

I laugh and take a look around. The whole place is untouched. The trash cans reek. It's dark inside, but no place is darker than the kitchen behind the front counter. Chris twirls the Bowie knife around a few times and jumps over the counter.

I crawl after him. I don't want him to reach the freezer before I do. If there are hash browns in there, I claim them all. I flick on the flashlight we took from the thugs last night and shine it around the kitchen. Fetid remains of food have been scraped across the floor. Black, dirty footprints mar the tile. All the signs of mass panic.

"There's the freezer," I say, pointing to a steel box in the wall. "Let's raid it!"

"Don't get your hopes up," Chris warns. "It's been a week since the electricity went out. If there's anything in there it's probably rotten."

"Party pooper," I snap.

I keep the flashlight trained on the freezer as I tap the door. It's halfway open. I frown. "Go ahead already," Chris says.

"I'm going, I'm going."

I open the door and look inside, seeing a series of empty steel shelves and melted icepacks. There are several packages of hamburger meat in the back corner. They smell heinous – rotting. "Gross," I say, shutting the door. "Great. It's back to energy bars again."

"Tried to tell you," Chris shrugs.

"Forgive me for holding out some hope that there was still junk food left in the world."

"You've got some of the most unorthodox hopes."

"I do not."

"Yes, you actually *do*."

"You could have hope for world peace."

"Who gives a crap about world peace? I want French fries."

"See? I rest my case."

Ding.

We both shut up. Stop talking, stop moving. Something metal hits the tile of the kitchen flooring and makes a noise like a bell. I whip my flashlight around, spotting a metal spoon spinning on the floor.

"What the...?"

A shadow moves across the back of the kitchen, headed for the rear door. I hear light footsteps. Chris immediately vaults over the counter and tackles the shadow. I scurry after him, buzzing with adrenaline.

How many times are people going to sneak up on us?

I shine the flashlight and wrinkle my nose. Chris is holding a skinny kid by the shoulders. A girl. She's got scraggly blonde hair, knee-high combat boots and fingerless gloves. "Wow," she says, appearing angry. "You just tackled me. Classy. Let go, will you?"

She kicks Chris in the leg. It doesn't hurt him, but he lets go anyway.

"Geez," I say. "You're just a kid."

"You and me both," she shrugs, turning to face me. Her skin is extremely pale, almost cherubic. She looks around eleven or twelve. "What's up with the sacking theatrics?"

"Sorry," I say. "We thought you were dangerous."

"I am," she sniffs. "Anyway, this is *my* McDonald's."

"Where are your parents?" Chris asks.

"Wouldn't you like to know?" She only comes up to my shoulder. "Hellooo. Leave. Now."

"Answer the question," I say, crossing my arms.

"Where are *your* parents?" she asks, raising an eyebrow.

"Are you alone?" I press. "Who's taking care of you?"

"I can handle myself," she answers, looking proud. "Bye."

She turns to leave, but Chris catches her around the waist and holds her there. "You're alone," he states. "How long have you been hiding out here?"

The girl tries to wrestle herself out of Chris's grip, but not even a sumo wrestler could break those iron arms. "I don't know. A week, maybe? Everybody left when the electricity went out. I came here to find food."

"Why didn't your parents take you with them?" I ask, appalled.

"I don't *have* parents," she replies. "I'm a foster child, okay?"

I sigh.

"I get it." I look around the kitchen. "So. Is there any food left?"

"Like I would share it with *you*," she snorts.

Chris gives her his death stare. She swallows.

"Fine," she says. "This way."

She shoves past me and tromps into the other half of the kitchen. She opens a sliding door underneath the counter and pulls out a few boxes of cookies and sealed apple slices.

"Happy now?" she demands.

"What's your name?" I ask, dumping a handful of apple packages into my pack. "How old are you?"

"Twelve. Almost thirteen," she replies, picking at a cookie.

"And your *name*?" I say, placing my hands on my hips.

"Isabel," she replies.

"I'm Cassidy," I smile, shaking her hand whether she wants me to or not. "And this is Chris."

"He your boyfriend?" Isabel asks.

I flush, glad I can't see Chris's face.

"He's my *friend*," I reply. "Do you have any family or friends around here who can help you?"

"No. The whole area's empty," she shrugs. "I got left behind."

"How?"

"My foster family left without me." She bites down on a cookie, propping her legs up against the wall. "There are like, two people in the whole county around here so it's not like it took long for everybody to disappear."

"Have you been living off cookies and apples for a week?" I ask.

"There were French fries and hamburgers and stuff at first," she answers. "Then the food started getting nasty."

"Yeah, that's pretty much what's happening everywhere." I turn to Chris, who's putting a few cookies in his backpack. "Don't overdo it there. Chocolate melts."

He stuffs one more in his bag before shooting me a you-can't-tell-me-what-to-do look. I turn back to Isabel.

"Look, we can't leave you here alone," I say. "We're headed north. You can come with us."

Behind me, Chris heaves a sigh.

"She's a *kid*," he mumbles.

"She's coming with us," I say, making it clear that I won't take no for an answer. I'm not going to look back on my life a hundred years from now and have to remember that I left a twelve year-old girl in the middle of an empty McDonald's when the world ended.

"Seriously?" she says, surprised. "I can come with you?"

"Sure," I smile. "You'll be safe with us."

"That's debatable," Chris remarks.

"Shut up, Chris."

Isabel suddenly jumps forward and hugs me around the waist. It startles me, since only a minute ago she was kicking Chris in the shins. Then again, I would be a little defensive, too, if I'd been hiding in a dark kitchen for a week.

"Okay," I say, squeezing her shoulders. "We should move. You up for this?"

"Totally!" she beams. "Where are you going?"

"The mountains," I answer. "It's safe there."

"That's also debatable," Chris says.

131

"Hey, I found these, too," Isabel says, pulling open another drawer. There are some small water bottles inside. "Want some?"

"Water!" I exclaim. "Awesome. Good job, Isabel."

We fit as many as we can into our packs. Isabel stuffs a few into a backpack she pulls from underneath the counter. It's pink. *Hot* pink. "Nice," I comment.

"Thanks," she replies. "It's for school. I'm in sixth grade. Well...*was.*"

"Wow." We hop over the front counter, leaving McDonald's. The fog isn't as dense as it was during the early morning, but it's still cold. And wet. And depressing.

"I haven't been outside since it happened," Isabel remarks, somber. "There were a lot of weird people hanging around for a few days."

"What kind of weird people?" Chris asks.

"Bad people," she replies, chewing on her lower lip. "They stole the money from the cash register. Then they left. I didn't want to go outside because I thought they might still be there."

"That was a good idea," I say, sharing a concerned glance with Chris.

She kicks a rock down the road. "So where are we going again?"

"The mountains," I repeat. "There won't be bad people there."

"Cool. Do you have, like, a secret fortress or something?"

"Or something."

"Why won't you tell me?"

"When you need to know, I'll explain it to you, okay?"

"Okay," she sighs. "So Cassidy.... are you in high school?"

"No. College." I tilt my head. "Chris was a Navy SEAL."

132

"A Navy *Seal*?" she laughs. "What's *that*?"

I raise my eyebrows at Chris. He shifts the rifles and the backpack before launching into a convincing explanation about the awesomeness of his former SEAL team. Even I get into it.

"The question is," I say, "have you ever worn a tuxedo under a wetsuit? It's the ultimate smooth move."

Unfortunately, he's never tried that.

Isabel asks, "Cassidy, do you have parents?"

"Kind of."

We walk to the freeway, reverting to car counting and complaining about the weather. Only now we have a twelve year-old cutting into the conversation, talking almost non-stop about school and math and her many friends.

Mid-morning rolls around, leaving us sleepy. Except for Isabel, who seems to have endless energy and an incessant need to engage in constant conversation.

"Hey," I say, around ten o'clock. "What's that?"

We slow down, spotting dark shapes in the distance.

"Probably just some more cars," Isabel yawns.

"Maybe."

Chris drops behind her and tosses me one of the rifles.

"I can't shoot one of these," I say.

"Then hold it to keep up appearances," he replies. "Just in case."

I don't argue. Frankly, I'm too tired. Tromping along for miles *and* having to keep up a conversation with a tween is burning me out. As we get closer to the dark shapes, we stop talking.

Even Isabel closes her mouth.

There's something...off.

I keep a firm grip on the rifle. I'm not entirely sure how to use it. Chris knows how, though, so I let him walk out front. I'll be the moving target if something goes wrong.

Noble of me, I know.

"Guys," Isabel shrieks.

Startled by her voice, I jerk backwards, turning back to scowl at her. "Be *quiet*," I say.

"Look!" she points.

I follow her finger. Only after a few seconds do I finally make out the shape of an upright vehicle. Then three. Four. Five. All pointed south on a freeway where the vehicles were headed north.

I know what this is:

"It's a roadblock."

Half-visible figures get out of the vehicles. Car doors slam. Voices. Yelling. I shout, "RUN!" to Isabel, and she doesn't hesitate. She takes off into the fog and disappears before I can even remind her to stay close to me. Chris backs up a few steps and puts his hand on my arm.

"Catch up to her," he breathes. "Go."

We break into a dead sprint. Footsteps – loud and close – echo behind us. "STOP!" a man yells.

Right. Like I'm going to do *that*.

Then, out of nowhere, someone tackles Chris. He tumbles to the ground and rolls back up to his feet, yelling at me to keep going.

"Don't stop!"

I hesitate, spotting the guy who tackled him. He's wearing an Omega uniform. We lock eyes. His gaze is menacing.

Somebody tackles *me* this time. I hit the road, hoping I don't break something, and scramble to my feet. A guard with beady eyes and thick muscles hauls me backwards and locks his arms around my upper body. I kick against him, jamming my elbows into his stomach with all my might. He loosens just enough for me to wriggle away and kick him in the mouth.

He falls hard. Another assailant grabs me from behind. Beady Eyes climbs to his feet and wrestles me to the ground. Now I have *two* guys on top of me. I can't see or hear Chris. I kick and scratch and bite and punch. It doesn't do much good. I'm pinned.

Totally, completely pinned.

"What's this?" Beady Eyes says, ripping my backpack off. Dislocating my shoulder in the process. *Thanks a lot.* "Supplies? Where are you going?"

"Get off me," I grit, struggling for breath. "Let me *up!*"

"Not so fast," he replies, smug. "You know why we have this roadblock? To keep people from getting out of town so easily. So many people follow the freeways to get out. You can't just leave, you know. It's not legal."

"I'll do whatever the hell I want," I shout. "This is a free country." Mr. Beady Eyes breaks into a grim smile.

"You only think it is."

And then everything goes black.

Major bummer.

When I was six years old, I had an argument with my mother. I vaguely remember holding a glass of water in my hand at the time, and then promptly dumping that water in her face. Granted, that was a stupid move, but I young. I also had a bad temper.

My dad came home the next morning. I was punished, forced to sit in the corner of my room, unable to watch television or read a book. All I can remember is that I was frustrated. Because no matter what I said, I wasn't allowed to go *anywhere* until the two hours were up. It was embarrassing.

I never threw water in Mom's face again.

When I wake up, I'm looking at a corner again. My cheek is pressed against scratchy carpet and my head is ringing, pounding. Yes. My old friend the headache is back. Again.

I sit upright and look around, seeing nothing but a bright fluorescent light coming from the back of the room.

Wait. *Room?*

I refocus. I'm in a hotel room. But there is no furniture. No bed, no chairs, no TV or TV stand, no nothing. It's totally empty. The bright light is coming from above the hotel room sink, right outside the bathroom.

I hobble to my feet, feeling unsteady, calling, "Chris? Isabel?"

Apparently I'm alone. Then it all comes back to me: the roadblock, Beady Eyes…crap. What did they do to me? I feel a line of dried mud along the top of my forehead. When I rub it between my fingers I realize that it's not mud – it's *blood*. I approach the mirror and stare at the tiny, redheaded girl gazing back.

She looks like she got run over by a truck.

I splash cold water on my face and scrub the blood away, wondering where my backpack is. And my pain meds. I don't think I can take much more of this headache.

What's wrong with me? How sick am I?

I walk over to the door and try pulling it open. No dice. It's locked. The windows are covered with black tarp. I try to tear through. Not happening.

I bang on the door a few times. Then I kick it. I sit down in the middle of the empty room and pick at the carpet.

Screech...

I look up as the door opens. A beam of light falls across the floor. An Omega guard walks in. It's my old enemy: Beady Eyes. He's wearing the same blue uniform with a white O stitched on the sleeve. He's also alone. I get a glimpse of an outdoor hallway and railing before he shuts the door.

"Sleep well?" he asks, flashing a calculating smile. He's got a German accent.

"Yeah, I did," I reply, folding my arms across my chest. "Where am I? Where are my friends?"

He just smiles, squatting down so he's at eye-level. Not something I find appealing. At all.

"Why don't I ask the questions?" he purrs. "What is your name?"

"Anne of Green Gables," I say.

"Where are you *from*?" he demands.

"Canada. Where the moose live."

"Give me real answers," he hisses. He no longer smiles.

"Those were real."

"I mean the *truth*."

"Oh, that," I click my tongue against my teeth, hoping he won't be able to tell how scared I am. "Why don't you start? Like, why is

137

Omega killing innocent civilians? And what do you know about the electromagnetic pulse?"

He slowly stands up, his eyes going from beady to steely.

"You are a stupid fool," he spits. "Like most of the people in this country. No one ever saw it coming. *You* didn't. Or *did* you?" He raises a finger. "You have supplies. You were headed north on foot. You were avoiding the relief camps. Why?"

"Maybe because the relief camps are more like kill zones," I say, expressionless. "My idea of relief isn't being shot in the chest."

"Your traveling companion, the soldier," he continues, ignoring my answer, "is well-trained. The two of you together were planning something, weren't you?"

"Planning what? A diabolical plot to steal the rest of the fast-food along the interstate?" I roll my eyes. "You're an idiot."

Quicker than I can see, his hand lashes out and he strikes me across the face. I grab my head and grind my teeth together. Now my head *really* hurts.

I swear.

"I want to know where you and your companion were going," he demands.

And that's when I realize he used the word *companion*. Not plural, but single. Which means Isabel must have escaped.

"We were trying to find food and water," I say. "That's it."

"What about the supplies in your backpacks? And the weapons?"

"Never hurts to be prepared."

He looks like he's going to hit me again, but restrains himself.

"We are functioning under a State of Emergency," he drawls. "Martial Law prevails, and if you are somehow involved in a conspiracy against the relief effort, I promise you, I will get it out of you sooner or later."

"Conspiracy against the relief effort?" I echo. "You mean your executions?"

"You and I see things in different lights."

"Yeah. You're evil and I'm not. There's a difference."

"We will see how sarcastic you are after a week without food or water," he growls. "You may or may not survive."

"Yeah, yeah," I wave him off, but inside, I'm afraid. "Death, doom and destruction. Whatever."

He walks away and opens the door, slamming it shut behind him. Sliding the lock into place. I lie on my back and wrap my hands around the roots of my hair, trying to take the pain away. I can feel part of my face swelling up from Beady Eyes' slap in the face.

Seriously.

First the world ends, then I'm taken captive by maniacal relief workers turned murderers in the middle of an empty hotel room.

Nobody would believe this. Not even my dad.

The door opens again.

Has it been minutes? Days? Weeks.

I don't know.

I'm starving and, because the plumbing in the room doesn't work, dying for water. My lips are caked with dried blood. I can't swallow – there's no saliva left in my mouth. I can only breathe and conserve what little energy I have left.

Propped up against the wall, I open my eyes, watching a pair of black boots move across the carpet toward me. I look into the face of Beady Eyes.

"Come with me," he says simply.

I don't move. One, because I don't want to. And two, because I literally don't have the strength for it. Beady Eyes grabs me by the arm and yanks me to my feet. As I expected, the room swirls around me and my head throbs. I catch a glimpse of a name tag on Beady Eyes' uniform: *Keller.*

He marches with me in tow out the door, into an outdoor hallway. There's not much to see: a grimy traveler's motel, limited parking space, zero shrubbery. What interests me are the military vehicles in the parking lot. There are several. They're darkly painted. And in the center of the parking lot, a small bonfire is illuminating the property. It smells of burning garbage.

"Living the high life?" I ask, raising an eyebrow.

He grunts and drags me along.

We descend the stairwell, walk across the parking lot, and come to a glass door marked *Main Office.* I spot other soldiers standing around the bonfire before we walk inside. It's cold. It also smells like stale sardines, which is more than a little off-putting. Reminds me of a Motel 6 my dad and I once stayed at on the way to Yosemite National Park.

Good times.

The main office has a shelf of travel brochures on the counter. A clock on the wall is ticking *way* too loudly. Keller shoves me ahead of him. I catch myself. Regain my balance.

I see Chris.

I force my face to remain expressionless.

He's sitting in an office chair. There are four Omega guards standing around him, two of them have guns pointed at the back of his neck. He's a bruised, bloody mess. By the looks of it, his time here has been worse than mine.

"What's going on?" I ask. Chris and I lock eyes.

His jaw tightens as he takes in my appearance. I look bad. I know that. His eyes tell me that he's unhappy. *Very* unhappy.

Angry.

"Your companion would not tell us anything about himself," Keller says, leaning close enough to breathe on me. "His ID told us very little, only that he was in the military. Perhaps you can tell us more about the two of you and your plans?"

I glance at Chris. He nods slightly, only enough for me to catch.

"First of all," I say, putting my hand on the counter for support, "you're kind of a jerk. Second of all, I don't have a freaking idea what you're talking about. The world ended, okay? Everything died. We had to get out of the city because the radio stations were broadcasting that people should evacuate. That's what we did. We *left.*"

"This man is a highly trained ex-military operative," Keller yells, placing his hand on my arm. Squeezing tight. "The driver's license in *your* purse indicates that you're the daughter of Frank Hart, also a highly trained law enforcement officer and private detective. These are not coincidences."

"How do you know who my father is?" I demand. "It's not like you can Google it."

Keller smirks.

"Can't we?"

"You have computers?" I say, openmouthed. "How?"

"You tell me. You seemed to have anticipated the EMP. You avoided the relief camps while the rest of the populace was flocking to them. You had a vehicle that was protected from EMPs. You were even armed."

I stare at him. How does he know?

Only Dad and I knew about the Mustang. No one else.

It was our secret.

"You think we're rebels," I state. And then, "This invasion...how long has it been planned? Because if you're worried that *two* people are going to throw a wrench in your plans, maybe your strategy isn't as brilliant as you thought."

Keller reacts immediately, back-handing me across the face. Color explodes before my eyes. Hot, searing pain sizzles on my cheek. I instinctively hold my hand to my face, grimacing.

Chris grips the armrests of his chair. Tightly.

"Let her go," he growls. "Keep me if you want to, but she hasn't done anything wrong."

"We'll keep who we want," Keller snaps. "I have no sympathy for you. But you *do* have a choice. You can either comply with my wishes and tell me where you're going and what you know, *or* you can die. Two more deaths mean nothing to me. It's your choice. You may have a few moments to discuss."

He gestures to the guards.

"Don't attempt escape," he warns. "You'll be shot."

They walk outside, leaving us visible to them through the glass door. As soon as the door shuts, I throw my arms around Chris's neck and embrace him, holding back tears.

"You look terrible," I say, sniffling. "How bad are you hurt?"

Chris sinks to the ground and gathers me up in his arms, pressing me against his chest.

"I'm fine," he replies. "What did they do to *you*?"

"Keller's trying to starve me out."

I look up into his face, pressing my fingers against his cheek.

"How long has it been since they took us?" I ask.

"Four days," he replies. "Where are they keeping you?"

"Upstairs. The last door on the right. You?"

"In the back of one of their trucks." He offers a weak grin. "I guess they figured if they put me in a room I'd just break the windows out."

"You're good at that," I agree, resting my head against his shoulder. He smells sweaty and bloody, but honestly, I don't care. I don't think I've ever missed another human being as much as I've missed Chris in the last few days.

I felt...empty without him.

"They're going to kill us," Chris says at last, tilting my chin up. "You know that, right?"

I nod, swallowing a thick lump in my throat.

"I figured," I answer, shaking.

"I have a plan. We can escape."

"Excuse me?" I sit up straight, his arms still around my waist. "How?"

"Just trust me."

"But Chris –"

"-No buts, Cassidy," he says, placing one hand on each side of my face. "Just trust."

He runs his finger along my bruised eye and frowns, leaning forward. "I should kill him," he whispers. Anger sparks in his eyes.

"Don't say that," I reply softly.

But inwardly, I'm relieved. He wants to protect me.

He *cares.*

Chris rests his forehead against mine. We sit there, holding each other, eyes closed.

Sixty seconds.

Chris brushes my hair back. He presses his lips against my forehead. It's a short, lingering kiss. Soft and compassionate.

I forget to breathe.

"I'll take care of you," he says, thumbing my cheek a final time.

I nod, loving the way his hands are warm against my face.

Ding.

The bell on top of the office door jingles as Keller re-enters. The guards are with him.

"How sweet," Keller says in mock sugariness.

Chris stands up, pulling me to my feet. I lean on him for support. I'm too weak to stand on my own. I can barely speak.

"Aw, thank you," I reply. "Almost as adorable as you and your cronies?"

But apparently I can manage sarcasm *just* fine.

Keller's face turns ashen gray.

"You're going to wish you hadn't said that," he grits, "before the night is over."

"I don't think so," I say.

Chris tightens his grip around my waist.

"If you touch a hair on her head," he says calmly, "I will make your death long and painful."

Keller rolls his eyes.

"So theatric," he complains. "I take that as a sign that you're not going to tell me what I want to know?"

"No," I reply.

*Not like we **have** any information to give away...*

"It's your funeral, not mine," Keller spits. "Fine."

"Cassidy," Chris says, looking at me. "Duck."

"Hmm?"

Chris pulls me to the ground.

Something – it *sounds* close – explodes. I feel heat on my skin. Orange flames blast the office. Glass shatters. Men shriek. Hot debris scatters across my back, peppering my clothes. I slowly raise my head. The scene seems to move in slow motion.

I see a giant fire outside – way bigger than the bonfire that the soldiers were hanging around earlier. It looks like some of the vehicles have been turned upside down from whatever detonated.

"Come on!" Chris yells, wrapping his hand around mine. "We have to move!"

Well, obviously.

I get up, forgetting my health issues thanks to a rush of good old-fashioned adrenaline. Chris throws the door open and I'm hit in the face with a wave of heat. I cover my face, guarding my skin from being burned. The flames are monstrous.

145

"What happened?" I shout, following Chris's lead through the wreckage. Two Humvees are completely flipped over. Several troops seem to be stuck inside. I feel bad, then I remember that these people are trying to *kill* us.

Priorities: Rearranged.

Omega guards are staggering, struggling to stand upright. The shockwave from the explosion has temporarily destroyed their sense of balance.

You and me both, pals.

Chris and I run to the other side of the motel. There are no soldiers here. Only one vehicle, a Humvee with an Omega insignia on the side: The O that doubles as a white globe.

And leaning against the Humvee with a pair of keys in her hands is Isabel. She is infuriatingly casual.

"Took you long enough," she comments.

"What did you do?" I say, spaced. Puzzled. "How are you here?"

"I dumped gasoline on the fire. A *lot* of gasoline." She shrugs. "Right, Chris?"

"You did a good job," he says, slapping her on the back. Then he takes the keys and opens the door. "Get inside. Now."

"How did you coordinate this?" I ask, climbing across the console in the front seat. Isabel jumps into the back, a storage area of guns, ammo and emergency supplies. "Holy crap! We hit the jackpot!"

"It's Keller's car," Isabel grins.

"No way?" I laugh. "Even better."

Chris turns the key in the ignition. The engine roars to life.

"Yes!" Isabel whoops. "It works!"

I breathe a sigh of relief.

Chris is stoked. He floors it, and we're out of here.

"I saw where they took you," Isabel tells me, picking up an AK-47.

"Put that *down*," I say, taking it out of her hands. Putting it back. She makes a face.

"I found Chris, and the truck they were keeping him in had a window," she continues. "I snuck over. We made a plan. I knew where you were going to be." She smiles devilishly. This girl is only *twelve*? "He told me to throw one of the gas canisters in the fire and run. I found *way* more than one, though. That was the best explosion *ever*!"

"Unbelievable," I say, reaching around for a hug. "I'm *so* glad we found you! I knew you'd come in handy. I told you, Chris."

"I believe the gasoline was my idea."

"Yeah, but *she* pulled it off."

"Thanks to me."

"People, the *road*!" Isabel screams.

Chris swerves, narrowly missing a car that's sitting horizontally at an intersection. We're racing full speed through the dark country roads, one orchard after another flashing by my window. It's not terribly foggy. Thank goodness.

Foggy enough to hide us, but not too foggy that we can't drive.

"They're going to hunt for us," Chris says. "They have our stuff. They'll try to figure out where we were going."

"Why?" I say, kicking the door. "We never did anything to them."

"We're anomalies," Chris shrugs. "They think we're trying to fight against the new regime."

"Maybe we are," I say bitterly. My adrenaline is draining away. The uncertainties – and the headache – are coming back. "How did

Keller know we had the Mustang? How did he know who my dad was?"

"Apparently there's still some Internet access that the government's got going for their boys," Chris replies, knitting his brow. "Which means we were right, Cassie. This was an inside job. Somebody on *our* side did this to us. Or at least contributed to it."

I rest my head against the seat, exhausted.

"So what do we do?" I say. "We have their car. Will they be able to track us somehow?"

"I don't think so," Chris muses. "Wherever their computer is, it's in a truck somewhere and it's probably got limited connection to a satellite."

"So we're safe?" Isabel asks, leaning between our seats.

"Yeah," I say. But it's only a half-truth. "We're okay right now."

She sighs and leans her head against my shoulder.

"Awesomesauce."

Chapter Ten

Around dawn, I see it. The foothills. I whoop for joy and Isabel joins in. Chris just smiles. Satisfied.

"We should get some kind of blue ribbon for getting this far," I say. "Who's with me?"

"I'm *with* you," Isabel agrees, giving me a high-five.

"Chris?" I ask, grinning.

"Fine. A blue ribbon for everyone." He shifts in the driver's seat, stiff from hours of navigating the back roads. It took a long time to get here, to find our way through the hundreds of twists and turns of the country highways. I've officially seen parts of the Central Valley that I never want to see again.

Ever.

Currently, we're coasting down a stretch of Highway 180, the gateway to Kings Canyon and Sequoia National Park. Epic win. We have enough gas in the tank to get us to Chris's parents' home, which is somewhere outside of Squaw Valley.

That's assuming we actually make it there.

After Chris finds his family, I'm not sure what I'm going to do. Continue to the cabin by myself, I guess. Dad will be expecting me.

*I **have** to be there...*

"So what are your parents like?" I ask, turning to Chris.

"They're farmers," he replies.

"That's it? Come on, I've got time to listen."

"They'll like you," he says, eyes twinkling. "My dad's a little rough around the edges... My brother will *love* you." He visibly cringes as he utters the last sentence.

"Oh, so he *is* single," I answer coyly. "Did you hear that, Isabel? Chris's brother is *single*."

"Praise the *Lord*," she drawls.

"What's his name?" I ask.

"Jeff," Chris replies, annoyed. "And he's seventeen. He's too young for you."

"I'm *nineteen*," I answer. "That's a two year age difference. Who cares?"

"Yeah, well...he's not your type."

"Not my type?" I giggle. "You have no idea what my type is."

"Neither do you," he whispers.

I laugh softly, pressing my fingers against my forehead. God, my head really hurts. The vision blurs around the edges. I take a deep, shaky breath. And I begin to cry. Just like that. They slip down my face. My hands tremble. The world spins. The pressure builds.

I have never felt like this before.

"Cassidy?" Chris asks. "Whoa. Cassie? What's wrong?"

"Yeah, what's wrong?" Isabel echoes, poking her head up front.

"I don't know," I whisper. "Something's...not right."

Understatement.

I focus on deep breathing. It's not helping. The tears continue to flow, and the pain becomes acutely intense.

"Relax, Cassie," Chris keeps saying. "Relax. It's okay. Take a deep breath. This isn't the end of the world. Ah, okay, it *is*, but we're alive, right?"

"Chris," I say.

He casts an anxious glance at me.

"I'm going to puke," I state matter-of-factly, feeling nauseas. "Like, right now!"

I slap my hand over my mouth. Chris slams on the brakes and eases to the side of the road. I throw the door open and jump outside, the cold air stinging my cheeks. I kneel and vomit on the gravel.

What's happening to me?

Chris rolls across the seat, steps outside and kneels beside me, holding my hair away from my face. He rubs my back, drawing comforting circles against my shoulders. I'm shivering. Cold.

"Cassidy, look at me," Chris says, turning my face toward him. "You're sick. Okay? That's all. You're going to be fine."

The lines of his face are tight. I dry-heave and look down at the gravel, horrified. It's bloody.

I'm vomiting blood.

"What's wrong with me?" I ask.

And this time, I am afraid.

He adjusts his stance and tightens his grip on my arms.

"I don't know," he says honestly. "But my mom will."

"Your...mom?" I murmur.

"Yeah. She used to be a nurse. Did I mention that?"

"Mmm...no."

"Huh." Chris scoops me up into his arms. Sick as I am, I appreciate the warmth of his body heat. "Hang in there, kid."

Isabel opens the rear door and Chris lays me flat against the floor in the backseat. The scenery is spinning. Noises are abnormally loud. Painful. I squeeze my eyes shut. When I open them again, I see streams of sunlight coming through the windshield. Isabel peers at my face like a curious cat.

"Are you still alive?" she asks.

I blink, shaking my head.

"She says she's not alive," Isabel says, looking over the front seat.

I fade out before I catch Chris's reply. If it's possible to feel any worse than I do now, the pit of my stomach cramps. I slide my hand under my shirt and pull it upwards, glimpsing my bruise from crowbar boy in Santa Clarita. It's black and blue, veins of red running throughout the injury. It's also painful to the touch.

When did *that* happen?

"Guys…" I slur.

I can't seem to find the energy to form a sentence. My heart sounds strangely loud, as if it's trying to escape my chest. That's not right. Why am I sinking? Why can't I hold onto my thoughts? They slip through my fingers like wisps of smoke.

I am falling.

I am asleep.

Who would have believed that just a couple of weeks ago, my biggest problem was getting an employment rejection from an airline company? Now *everything* is gone. Stuff like that doesn't matter anymore. Money doesn't matter. College degrees don't matter. Whether or not you saw the latest Oscar-winning film doesn't matter.

All that matters is one thing:

Are you still alive?

I wake up. I feel numb, as if hundreds of tiny needles are pricking my skin. I've only felt this sensation once, when I broke my arm and I had to go to the hospital to set it. But there are no more hospitals.

So where am I?

I force my eyes open. The first thing I see is a dark wood ceiling. There are two closed curtains. Sunlight pokes through the slits between the fabric. I'm lying on my back, tucked beneath a quilt.

How did I get into a *bed*?

I push myself up, surprised to notice that my headache is gone. Finally. I feel a little spacey, like I'm floating above everything in the room, but besides that...I feel *good*.

"Hello?" I say, but nothing comes out of my mouth. I clear my throat. "Hello?" No answer.

I peel the sheets back, noting what I'm wearing. A pair of flannel pajama pants and a white tank top. Who dressed me? I hope it was Isabel.

It *better* have been Isabel.

I swing my legs over the side of the bed, touching cold hardwood flooring. The room itself is rustic, with pictures and books and an old lamp covered with dust. I touch an antique dresser and spot a picture frame. I look it over. It's a picture of a rugged, handsome young man in a suit and tie. He bears a striking resemblance to Chris.

Hmm.

I turn it over. Someone has written *Chris, Senior Year*, in pencil on the back of the frame. I stare at it, then turn the picture over, smitten with the young man in the picture. Chris. Ten years ago.

And now he's got a beard, long hair and a tattoo of a cobra on his left bicep.

Nice.

I put the picture back and creep to the door. I know where I am now. We must have made it to Chris's family home. I open it and peek into a long, dark hallway. The architecture is miniature. Old.

I follow the hall. Every door is closed except for mine, which means I can't snoop. Bummer. I come to a stairway. Black and white photos line the wall here. Family pictures, I suppose.

I go downstairs.

There's an oak door. Windows are covered with curtains. On the left is a living room – a huge one with worn couches and an old television set – and on the right is a dining room with a hefty table. I can't hear any noises from anywhere in the house, so I turn and go back upstairs. Frankly, I may be feeling *better*, but I still feel tired. I yawn, walk back into the bedroom I was in, and crawl into bed. I pull the quilt around my shoulders, chilled. Obviously Chris and Isabel are here *somewhere*, I just have to wait for them to come back and get me.

"Knock, knock."

A tall, lean young man with blonde hair is standing in the doorway. He's wearing jeans and a plaid shirt, removing a pair of dirty gloves.

"Jeff?" I say, raising an eyebrow.

He grins. It's cute.

"Yeah, that's me," he replies "You're Cassidy."

"Where's Chris?" I ask. "And Isabel?"

"They're outside, helping the folks," he answers. "I'll tell them you're awake."

"Hey, wait!" I say, stumbling out of bed. "Listen, how long have I been here? What happened?"

"You've been out for about two days," Jeff replies. His eyes study the length of my body. I suddenly feel exposed. "My mom's a nurse. She helped you. She's got medicine and stuff she keeps for emergencies." He sticks his gloves in his back pocket, crossing his arms. Totally *ripped* arms, I might add. Not as strong as his older brother, but still. "You were really sick."

"Yeah, I know," I say, tugging on the ends of my hair. "What was wrong with me?"

"I think you were bleeding internally," he shrugs. "I mean, that's what my mom said. It must have been fixable, though." He beams. "Obviously."

I smile.

"Thanks for taking me in," I say. And I mean it. "I just...thank you."

"No problem," he answers. "Chris has never brought home any friends before, let alone any girls. Or pretty ones."

I blush. "I'd like to meet your parents," I say. "I need to thank your mom."

"Sure," he agrees brightly. "Why don't you come down to the kitchen? You gotta be hungry. Chris and Isabel ate a couple of tons of food when they got here."

"Sounds like them," I remark.

"Come on," he waves for me to follow him. "So you're nineteen, right?"

"Yeah." We walk down the hall, to the stairs. "And you're seventeen. A senior."

"Like that matters anymore," he sighs. "I think the school year kind of froze when the pulse hit."

"Tell me about it." We reach the bottom of the stairs and walk into the kitchen. It's a cute room with big counters and lots of cupboards. "Where were you when it happened?"

"Home. The power went out," he answers. "Besides that, we didn't know anything was wrong. Until they started evacuating Squaw Valley. They tried to get us to leave, but we just kept stalling. They left us behind. Good thing, too. Chris told us about the Omega relief camps."

Jeff rummages through the cupboards and pulls out a bowl of apples and a bag of potato chips. "Might as well eat them before they go bad," he shrugs.

"Thanks!"

I pop open the bag and start eating. It's wonderful.

So much better than a protein bar.

"Chris told us that you're meeting your father at a cabin higher up," Jeff says, watching me eat.

"Yeah, that's the general plan," I answer, meeting his gaze. His eyes aren't quite as green as his brother's, but there's a certain amount of intensity that's the same. "But honestly, I don't know if he'll even be there."

"Never break an emergency plan," Jeff advises, leaning against the counter. "You should go."

I cock my head.

"Yeah, you're right," I agree. "I guess I'm just worried that he never made it out of L.A."

That maybe he's stuck in a concentration camp somewhere.

I shudder and grab another chip. "You have no idea how good this greasy crap tastes," I say. "I've been living on energy bars for a week."

Jeff chuckles.

"I understand that."

"So do I."

Both of us turn at the same time. Chris walks into the room. He's wearing dark-wash jeans, boots and a tight black tee under an open tan shirt. His hair is hanging loose, and he looks like he's been sweating it out doing something physical.

It's a *really* good look for him.

"Hey," I say. "We're still alive."

"*You're* still alive," he corrects, wrapping his arms around me. He pulls me into a warm, fantastic hug. I lay my head against his chest and breathe deeply. He rests his chin on top of my head. I don't even remember that Jeff is in the room until he says, "Where's Mom and Dad?"

"In the barn," Chris replies, gently easing away from me. He doesn't remove his arm from around my waist, though. Score. "My mother's going to want to check up on you, Cassie."

"Good, I want to meet her."

He studies my face for a long minute. "How do you feel?"

"Better. Did you run into any trouble while I was unconscious in the car?"

"No, we were lucky," he says. "Omega must have cleared out the whole town, because they didn't leave anybody behind. There's not enough of a population here to warrant their time."

He slides his hand on top of mine and brings it back down to my side.

"I need to talk to you." He glances at Jeff. "Privately."

"You and your *private* chats," Jeff huffs. "Why do I have to go?"

"Just get out of here," Chris replies.

Jeff ignores his brother and squeezes my shoulder.

"Glad to see you up, Cassidy," he says shyly.

"Thanks."

He exits the kitchen, mouthing something to Chris that I don't catch. Chris looks annoyed, but the hard lines of his face relax once his little brother leaves the room.

"Okay," I say. "So what's the scoop?"

"Have you been outside?" he asks.

"No. I just got up."

He folds his arms.

"We're almost thirty miles out of town," he says. "Most people have evacuated. I think we're safe here for a long time."

"What's your point?"

"My point? My *point* is that I think you should reconsider heading up to your cabin. Stay here, you'll be taken care of."

"I can take care of myself."

That's always been my first instinct. Denial.

I never ask for help.

"You need *help*," Chris replies. "Obviously. You were hemorrhaging internally, did Jeff tell you that? You've been bleeding every day since you got beaten in Santa Clarita."

"That would explain the headaches," I say.

"If you hadn't had pain meds, you wouldn't have lasted as long as you did," he says. "My mom was able to help you, but you'll be weak for a few days. Maybe even a couple of weeks. You need to rest and by the time you're even ready to head up the hill, it'll be snowing."

"So? I'll take a sled and a couple of Huskies," I quip.

"You know what I mean." Chris narrows his eyes. "You're not hiking forty miles to a cabin by yourself, Cassidy."

"I'm not?" I wilt. "I don't have a choice. My dad's waiting for me."

"You don't know that. And there's no reason you should die trying to get there. Wait it out. Go up in the spring." He grabs my arm as I make a move to walk away. "Your dad would want you to be safe."

"You don't know my dad," I reply, shaking him off. "This is the master plan, Chris! This was what we were supposed to do if an emergency happened and we got separated! The only reason I left L.A. was because we agreed on it. Otherwise I would have stayed."

"If you had stayed you would have died, just like thousands of others," Chris states.

I run a hand through my hair. *Dirty* hair.

"Can we discuss this later? I'm tired."

"Discussing it later won't change anything."

"You're right. I'm not going to change my mind on this."

"Cassidy, I just don't want you to get hurt."

"I survived this far," I say. "I can make it to the cabin. That was always the plan, and I'm going to carry it out. And by the way, I'm not going to die doing it."

Chris cringes when I use the word *die*.

I turn away and climb the stairs, upset. He's not my brother. He's not even my *boyfriend*. When it comes right down to it, I have to put the needs of my father before anyone else's.

Chris doesn't bother trying to follow me upstairs.

He knows I'm done discussing this.

But my mood soon lifts.

Chapter Eleven

It's taken the collapse of society for me to make friends. Growing up, I had an acquaintance or two, but no one I could really confide in. My mother worked. My father worked. My outlets were limited.

I was shy. I didn't make friends easily. I was my own best friend, and if I needed someone to talk to, I was on my own.

Life was lonely.

So, yeah, it's interesting that now I've got Isabel, Jeff, Chris and their parents as my buddies. The Young property is nestled on the backside of a foothill, hidden behind trees and fields of grass. A creek runs through a small canyon at the bottom of the property, where the whole place is fenced in with barbed wire.

The Young house has two levels. It gives off an old-fashioned, farmer vibe. There's a barn with a couple of cows and horses, a handful of chickens and pigs. Mrs. Young has raised a gorgeous vegetable garden behind the barn.

In other words, we're living in a survival junkie's paradise.

Mrs. Young is a short, slender woman with gray hair. She wears high-top jeans and plaid button-ups along with rubber boots. She's a sweet woman, if not a little tough. I suppose living with three rough-and-tumble men would give you a hard edge.

Mr. Young is similar in appearance to his sons. He's got overgrown graying hair, and he doesn't waste time making small talk. He's a man of few words. He's all business. All common sense.

It's been one day since I've woken up and Jeff has been showing me around the property. I'm wearing my jeans and boots with one of Mrs. Young's button-ups. I feel a little shaky, but overall much steadier.

"Hey..." I say, grinning. "What an ego trip."

A colorful rooster struts across the dirt in front of the barn.

"He reminds me of some guys I used to know," I say. "Show-offs."

"Were they really that bad?" Jeff asks.

"Yeah. Stuck-up city boys." I stroll along, plucking a leaf off an oak tree that's hanging low. "They weren't my type, let's put it that way."

"What? They just weren't your type or dating wasn't your thing?" Jeff trails behind me like a puppy. He's been doing that ever since Chris and I had our argument in the kitchen.

"You're a legal adult, though," Jeff says. "You *could* date, right?"

"I *can*," I correct. Then, "Why do you care?"

"I don't," Jeff replies quickly. "I was just curious. You know, my mom never let Chris go out with girls when he was growing up, and he had women all over..." he trails off, noticing my glare.

I don't need a detailed history of Chris's past love life.

"Anyway, they don't let me go out much, either," he says. "They're all about working hard until I turn eighteen, then I get to do what I want. Chris joined the military when he turned eighteen." He sighs. "Doesn't look like that's what I'll be doing anymore."

"Hey," I say, nudging his shoulder. "You know what you got?"

He shakes his head.

"You're alive," I exclaim. "You know how many people are dead or starving right now? We've got it made. We're living in the lap of luxury compared to some of them. Cheer up."

"You have a point," he admits. "I can see why my brother likes you."

I shift uncomfortably.

"Yeah?" I hesitate. "You think he likes me?"

"I know he does." Jeff shrugs. "I mean, he wouldn't have stuck with you for a week if he didn't. Believe me. I know."

"Huh."

A dirt road curves up the side of the foothill, right to the house. It's extremely well-hidden from the main highway. Mr. Young told me that when he saw the Omega troops rolling through, he knocked down his mailbox and camouflaged the entrance to the turnoff with bushes and trees.

"Chris told me you were in a charter school," I say as we walk into the barn. It's a large, spacious building. It smells of straw and livestock. I like it.

"Yeah," Jeff answers. "It was okay. At least I got to get off the property for a few hours every week."

I don't respond. If I lived here, with parents like his and a property like this, I don't think I'd care if I "got" to go to school. Then again, the grass is always greener on the other side. All I wanted growing up was a happy family.

Anyway, I'm sure Jeff has his own reasons for what he wants.

"Cassidy?"

I turn around. Chris walks into the barn with a box of tools in his right hand. He's hauling a couple of pieces of wood over his shoulder. "I'm fixing the leak in the roof," he announces. "Want to help?"

I think that's code for "Want to talk?"

I nod.

"Sure."

Jeff sighs, seeing that he's been dismissed from the conversation yet again. I smile apologetically but he waves it off. "See you later."

Chris is already halfway up the ladder.

"How do you do that?" I ask.

"What?" He climbs onto the loft and sets the tools down.

"Climb without using your hands. It's cool."

"Years of practice." I reach the top and step onto the creaky boards. There's a lot of straw up here, along with a gaping hole in the corner.

"What happened?" I say. "Did a meteor hit?"

"Nah. Just a couple of weak boards."

He begins working on patching it, removing his over-shirt in favor of the black tee. I lean back on the wall and watch him move, not realizing that I've been staring until he turns to me. "You're staring again, Cassie," he says, a wry grin spreading across his face.

"No, I'm watching you patch a hole," I reply, embarrassed. "There's not much else to do around here."

"Then don't watch," he says. "Do."

"Excuse me?"

He holds out a hammer.

"You use this while I hold this last piece of wood up. Can you handle that?"

"Duh," I reply. "If I can survive a week with you, I can do anything."

"Ha. Ha." He holds the last piece of wood up to the wall. "Go ahead."

I take the heavy hammer and pound it against the last nail. It's harder than it looks.

"Too much for you, Thumbelina?" Chris laughs.

"Shut up," I say, slapping his chest. "I can do it."

I pound a few more times. The nail is now halfway embedded into the wood. "There," I say, smug. "See?"

"You're hitting it at an angle," Chris replies, unimpressed. "That's why it won't go in all the way. Here."

He wraps his arms around me from behind and puts his hands over my hands. My body tenses with the close physical contact. An alarm bell goes off somewhere in my head.

"Swing back," Chris says, pulling my arms back, "and hit it head on."

He slams the hammerhead against the nail and it goes in all the way. In one sweep.

"Lucky shot," I shrug.

"Really?"

"Yeah. Really."

He draws one hand up my arm, fingering my long hair before tucking it behind my ear. "You know what I think?"

I shake my head, unable to move.

"I think you're stubborn."

"There's a newsflash for you."

His breath is hot against my cheek. He drops the hammer on the ground. "You also won't admit it when you can't do something," he says, and I can feel him smiling against my ear.

"So I have some pride," I whisper, curling my hands over the top of his, which are now resting on my stomach. "So what?"

"Nothing. I was just making an observation." He slowly kisses my neck, lingering just long enough to shift his position and brush his lips across the side of my cheek. He stops talking. So do I. I can think of nothing to say that would add to this moment.

I must be in love.

He kisses my other cheek, inching his hands up the side of my hips, careful to avoid my bruise. Then, without missing a beat, he tips my head to the right and leans in to press his lips against my forehead before dipping his head down. I close my eyes, forgetting about the nail and the hammer and the end of the world for a moment, and slide my hand around the back of his neck, bringing his lips down to mine.

I've never kissed a guy before, so I'm surprised at how easy it is to fall into. He tastes like coffee and smells even better, filling up every sense in my body.

Sensory overload.

Chris turns me around and presses me against his chest, his strong arms caging me in. There's no escape, and that knowledge sends a thrill through me. He's holding me so tight that I can barely breathe. I'm also substantially shorter than he is, so reaching him is an issue. I stand on tiptoes and pull myself up, wrapping my legs around his waist.

Chris holds me upright without flinching, slipping his hands under my legs, sinking down into the itchy straw. I break off the long kiss and rest my forehead against his. Chris is breathing hard – no harder than me, at least.

Both of us study each other, wordless. Chris's face is very relaxed, and he's smiling softly. He looks...*peaceful.*

I cup the side of his cheek with my hand, feeling the rough stubble under my fingers. I gently kiss him on the lips. He snakes his hand into my hair and returns the gesture before lying on his back, tracing his fingers over every angle of my face. He brushes his mouth across the hollow of my throat and I roll to his side, tucked underneath his arm and against his chest.

I toy with the fabric of his shirt for a few moments before he finally breaks the silence with his deep, strong voice. "I've been waiting to do that for a long time," he says, tracing my bottom lip with his thumb.

"Was it worth the wait?" I breathe.

"Absolutely. We should have done this sooner." He kisses me again, sending tendrils of electricity through my body. "Don't you agree?"

"I don't know." I prop myself up on one arm, still buzzing with the rush of such intimate contact. "Hey, you know what?"

"Hmm?"

"You're an older man."

"Meaning?" He raises an eyebrow.

"I'm nineteen. You're twenty-eight. This is practically illegal."

Chris sits up, laughing. It's a rich, seductive sound.

"Last I checked, nineteen was over the threshold of legal adulthood," he replies, pressing his mouth to my temple. "I think mutual consent is part of the equation."

"What if I don't consent?" I raise an eyebrow.

"I'll convince you," Chris says in a low voice.

167

"Do tell."

Chris chuckles and pulls me against him. I have to admit, if there's one positive thing about the EMP and the Omega takeover – it's definitely this.

For the next couple of days, I feel as if I'm floating on cloud nine. My health is almost completely back to normal. I spend my time helping Mrs. Young around the property, gathering chicken eggs – which are really breakable, by the way – cleaning the house and gathering and preserving food. At night we sit around the dining room table and eat together. We keep the curtains pulled tight so no light will escape. Of course, our lights are just lamps and candles, but still.

We don't want to give ourselves away.

Chris and Jeff have taken up a watch. Jeff stands guard for five hours during the night, then Chris, and then I finish out the early morning, watching for any signs of Omega or nomadic thugs. Chris usually stays with me for my so-called shift, which is a great opportunity for me to spend time alone with him. Every gesture, every touch and every word has a deeper meaning now that we've kissed. Now that he's made it obvious how he feels about me.

Living here is a simple, day-to-day existence that's all about routine. The best part? Everything is self-sustaining. Chickens, cows, horses, plants. All of this is what most people in the world – including myself if I hadn't run into Chris – are living without. No more fast food. No more sixty-second soup packages. No more ice cream bars. No more dieting. Instead we'll just have starvation and destruction.

Not exactly a stellar tradeoff.

About a week into my stay I'm sound asleep in bed. It's six a.m. I'm oversleeping. I usually rise at five-thirty to help Mrs. Young with the farm chores.

The door to my room creaks open. I awake immediately, because the sound is not a familiar one. Chris is standing in the doorway with his mother. He's wearing a tee shirt that reads "LIVE FREE OR DIE." His mother is wearing a red velvet dress.

I sit up, rubbing grit out of my eyes.

"Um...good morning?" I say. "Is something wrong?"

Mrs. Young beams.

"Merry Christmas!" she exclaims. "You forgot, didn't you?"

My jaw hits the floor. It can't be Christmas already...can it? I have never, *ever,* in the history of my life, forgotten about Christmas.

Apparently post-apocalyptic environments make me forgetful.

"No way!" I say. "I don't believe it!"

Chris walks to the bed, looking fantastic with his beautiful hair pulled back in a ponytail. His beard is still intact, but it's not very thick anymore. It's just right. He slips his hand behind my head and presses a quick, gentle kiss against my lips.

"Merry Christmas, Cassie," he says, eyeing me.

I blush for two reasons. First, because he kissed me. And second, because he kissed me in front of his *mother.*

"Thanks," I say.

"Come downstairs," Chris says. "You're going to love this."

I glance at Mrs. Young. She smiles at me – it's probably the nicest thing I've ever seen. So different from my own mother's smile.

Mrs. Young's smile is different. It's *real.*

I jump out of bed and pull on an old sweatshirt – compliments of Mrs. Young - and lace my fingers through Chris's. The three of us walk down the stairs, into the living room. The windows have been flung open. It's flipping cold in here but the floor furnace is warming things up. A fresh-cut Christmas tree stands in front of the window, and underneath it are several presents wrapped in cloth, tied with twine.

"Merry Christmas, Cassidy," Jeff says. He pulls me into a warm hug. When he doesn't let go, Chris shoves him in the shoulder. Needles to say, Jeff sits back down, but his goofy grin is still intact.

"Merry Christmas," I say, talking to Mr. Young.

He's wearing his beat-up jeans and work shirt, but his hair is combed. A first. He cracks a tiny smile – he's happy. He's not the most emotional person, so I take what I can get with him.

"I don't have anything for you guys," I say, embarrassed. "I totally forgot it was Christmas. I didn't even know what day it was."

"Don't worry about it," Mrs. Young assures me, sitting next to her husband. "We're just so glad to have you with us. You've been such a huge help around the farm."

I feel a bit of pride trickling into my chest.

"Thank you," I reply, happy. "For everything."

She nods.

Jeff jumps on the floor and tosses a present to Chris just as Isabel skips into the room, wearing a wool sweater and a beret.

Yes. A beret. *Really.*

"Merry Christmas, Cassie," she says, kissing me on the cheek. "I made you this."

She holds out a bouquet of flowers.

"Thank you," I say, giving her a hug. "I love it."

Jeff interrupts us by clearing his throat. We turn our attention back to the present he gave Chris. It's a long, thin box. "I got this for you months ago, bro," Jeff explains. "Been saving it."

Chris looks amused as he unfolds the cloth.

"Nice!" he says, impressed.

It's a hunting rifle. Jeff tosses a couple of boxes of ammo onto his lap. "I got you a couple thousand rounds. It's all in the attic."

"Thanks man," Chris says, giving his brother a hug. "We're going to need it."

Two boys bonding over ammunition. Classic.

"So what loot did you get me?" Jeff grins.

Chris pulls something from his pocket and flips it into Jeff's hands. I catch a glimpse of something shiny. Jeff holds it up. It's a ring.

"Man, this is your senior class ring," he says, looking completely shocked. "You can't give me this."

"Keep it," Chris replies. "Just because the world went to hell in a hand basket doesn't mean you shouldn't be allowed to graduate from high school."

Jeff's expression becomes more serious. He looks up at his brother, and I can see how much he idolizes him in just that one glance. "Thank you," he says, giving Chris a long hug.

I look at their parents. Mr. Young nods his head in approval. Mrs. Young, on the other hand, is dabbing at tears with a tissue.

"And for you," Jeff says, tossing me a long, slender box. "This is epic."

"Seriously?" I answer. "You didn't have to do this."

He shrugs.

I unwrap the cloth and pop open the box. There's a gorgeous, sharp knife with an ivory handle. I turn it sideways, looking at the carved inscription:

Cassidy Hart

I bite my trembling lip. Because I'm about to cry.

"Jeff, this is amazing," I say, knowing my voice is wobbly. "Thank you so much."

"You got it," he smiles. "I carved the handle myself. The knife came from this old shop they used to have downtown. I thought you could use it, since Omega took all your gear on the way up here."

I wrap my arms around his neck and hug him.

"You're awesome," I say, because I can't think of anything else to tell him.

"I know." He presses the knife against the palm of my hand. "I totally am."

I giggle. Chris rolls his eyes, and Mrs. Young stands up.

"I have Christmas breakfast, lunch and dinner," she announces. "Just because times are tough doesn't mean we can't celebrate the holidays." She puts an arm around each of her sons. "As long as we're all together, we have all we need. I love you boys. You know that, I hope."

Chris pulls his mom into a strong embrace. He kisses her cheek. "Yes, ma'am."

We eat a great breakfast of eggs, bacon, and homemade biscuits with some of Mrs. Young's raspberry preserves. No one works all day. We just kick back and enjoy Christmas. I spend most of my time listening to Chris and Jeff fool around with the new gun, but nobody's allowed to fire any shots in case dangerous individuals are roaming the area.

Later on, we eat an even more delicious dinner of roast chicken, fruit, rolls and salad. Every single piece of food on the table is from the Young farm. None of it came from a store. None of it was purchased.

At the end of the day, when I'm sitting in the window seat of my bedroom, watching the darkness set in, I have to admit: These are the kind of people that are going to survive this catastrophe.

"Cassidy?"

I turn. Chris walks into the room carrying a dinner roll in his hand.

"What? Seven rolls weren't enough for you?" I ask, raising an eyebrow.

"I like even numbers. Eight appealed to me."

"Don't appeal yourself right into obesity."

He tosses the roll up and down like a baseball and takes a seat next to me.

"What are you doing up here in the dark?" he asks, curious.

"Nothing. Just thinking."

"About...?"

"How amazing your family is." I sigh. "Really. Your family is...unbelievable. It's not that they're *just* nice people, it's this place. They're alive because they can do things for themselves. It's how life is supposed to be lived."

Chris doesn't answer for a long time. He stretches his legs across the window seat, leaning against the wall. "Society moved so far away from farming and self-sufficiency," he answers at last, "that a catastrophe like this will wipe out most of the country. Concentrated population spots are in the cities. The biggest death tolls will be in places like New York or Los Angeles."

I shut my eyes, thinking of my dad. And my mom.

"Hey," Chris says, nudging me with his boot. "You're safe here. That's all that matters."

"Yeah, but what about my dad?"

Chris remains silent. I can tell that he's trying to avoid talking about that. Last time we discussed it, it didn't go over very well.

Instead he reaches into his pocket and pulls out a gold chain.

"Here." He holds his hand out. I reach forward and open the palm of my hand. He drops the chain there. A small object is attached to it: A shield with a year on it, and on the back, Chris's name.

"What is it?" I ask.

"It matches the ring I gave Jeff." He picks it up and slips it over my head. "I want you to have it."

"Chris, I can't take this."

"Why not?"

"Because I'm not family. I can't."

"Cassidy," he says, fingering the necklace. "You *are* family now."

He leans back against the wall, looking straight into my eyes.

"Are you glad we met?" I ask.

"Yeah." He closes his eyes. "I'm glad."

I study his face in the shadowy candlelight of the room. He really is a beautiful man. A little rough around the edges, but I've always liked ruggedness. Without thinking, I lean over the length of the windowsill and kiss him, wrapping my arms around his neck.

He immediately slips his arms around my waist and presses me against his chest. I pull away and smile into the crook of his shoulder. "So…" I say, touching his arm. "What exactly does this cobra tattoo represent?"

I pull up his sleeve just enough to glimpse the ugly, vicious-looking head of the snake. "It obviously doesn't represent peace, love and good karma," I observe.

He kisses my forehead, sighing deeply.

"It's a Gadsden," he replies, stroking my hair.

"A *what?*"

"A Gadsden," he chuckles. "It's a snake. Common military tattoo."

"Bet your mom's gonna love that," I mutter, curling up against his chest.

"Yeah." He rests his head on top of mine, and we just stay there, until the wax from my bedside candle is pooling onto its glass plate.

It's such a perfect way to end Christmas day. But as I'm lying there in his arms, content and safe, I know deep down that this won't last. Because sooner or later, I'm going to have to leave this behind. I'm going to have to hike up to the cabin and find my dad.

That *was* the whole point of leaving L.A., after all.

Chapter Twelve

Something I've learned over the years – and particularly in the last few months – is that it never hurts to be prepared for the worst. Hope for the best, get ready for the crappy. Why not? It saved my life when the EMP hit the world.

So now I'm wrapped in three layers of clothing plus a heavy wool jacket. My hair is tied beneath a scarf and wide-brimmed hat; my fingers are covered with leather gloves.

I've got a backpack full of camping gear and first-aid supplies. And I'm standing on the edge of the Young's doorway, tears burning my eyes. Or maybe it's the cold weather. I don't know. I don't want to leave. I don't want to do this. But I have to – I *have* to get to the cabin to meet my dad.

I'm not afraid of the wilderness. Heck, I'm not even afraid of the dark like I used to be in Los Angeles. Pine trees and random squirrels just aren't as scary as thugs and Omega officers.

What I'm afraid of – and I mean *really* terrified of – is not doing the right thing. I can't abandon my dad just because it's easier – and safer – for me to stay here. Dad is counting on me, just like I'd be counting on him entirely if I hadn't met Chris or his family.

No, failing my father is somehow more scary than sleeping in the forest during the winter. Although I will freely admit that the thought of facing down a bear does make me want to walk a little faster.

I have to do this alone. Chris is safe, here, with his family. He's protecting them by being here, just like he protected me when we were escaping Los Angeles. He doesn't deserve the pain of a long hike on the cusp of winter. No. I'm doing this alone because I care about him. Because I want him to be happy.

I take a final glance at the Young property, a stillness washing over me. It's peaceful and silent at this early hour. No one has even gotten up to feed the chickens, yet. And somewhere in the house or in the barn, Chris is sound asleep, oblivious to the fact that I'm leaving.

A tear slips down my cheek, the first of many that are building up, threatening to spill onto my face. I'm suddenly afraid.

I kick the ground in frustration. If I cry, I'll lose my nerve.

I'll be back, I remind myself. *I'll tell Dad about the Youngs and we'll come back here together to help them with the farm. Then we can all be together.*

Even as I think it, I feel selfish. Here I am on a mission to make sure my dad is still alive and all I can focus on is getting back to the Young house – and Chris – as fast as I can.

I'm a regular Mother Theresa.

"Snap out of it," I tell myself, swallowing my hesitation. I physically tear my gaze away from the house and squeeze through the bushes, hacking a path down to the highway.

I'll be back...I'll be back...

That's what I keep repeating. Because the cold air is sharp against my skin, and the road seems a lot wider than usual. I guess I'm not used to walking alone. I pick up the pace. If I keep moving, I won't change my mind.

As I walk, the distance between the Young house and me heightens my anxiety. I'm not a tactical ninja like Chris. I can't find

177

food by looking under a rock. I can't wrestle wild animals with my bare hands.

I'm just a kid from L.A.

Caw!

My head snaps up. I spot a massive crow landing on top of a tree. He makes a few loud noises, hops onto a lower branch, and then swoops down onto the road.

"Good to know somebody's comfortable being out here," I mutter.

He gives me the eye.

I walk past him, feeling a little more relaxed once the first thirty minutes pass. This isn't so bad. There's no one around. It's peaceful here. If this is all it's going to take to get up to the cabin, it'll be like a walk in the park.

Figuratively speaking, of course.

I look over my left shoulder, a habit I picked up when Chris and I were trekking down the empty interstate out of Los Angeles. My chest tightens because there's nothing beside me but empty air.

I'll be back, I say for the fiftieth time. *He'll understand.*

After a couple of hours, the sun rises over the trees. The higher I get, the thicker the forest becomes, and as soon as I pass the snowline, everything begins smelling like wet dirt and sugar pine sap. Although it's obvious that there are no cars on the highway, I keep to the side of the road, ready to duck and roll into the pine needles if an Omega truck comes along.

At the four-hour mark, I stop and rest against a log that's fallen over the road. Nobody's going to bother to clear it. It's not like our taxpayer dollars are being used for useful things anymore.

I've brought some of Mrs. Young's food with me, like dried jerky and crackers. I've also got a few small canteens of water. I eat a small meal, pack it back up, and set off again.

It's boring walking through the woods without a companion to talk with, so I play games with myself to keep things interesting. Unfortunately, you can't really play "I Spy With My Little Eye" by yourself, and "Find That License Plate," is a no-go since there are no cars.

Mid-afternoon hits, and my feet are killing me. I'm well into the so-called "mountains," now, and I feel comfortable enough with the darker environment to take a breather out in the open. I lay down for about an hour, hydrate, and move on. When nighttime hits, I'm too frightened to navigate in the dark.

I don't want to end up walking off a cliff.

I make camp in a grove of fern at the base of a tree. I lay awake for a couple of hours, aware of every sound. Being in the middle of the woods is like sitting in a room that's so dark you can't see your hand in front of your face, only it's extremely cold, the ground is hard, and you have no idea what might be sneaking up behind you.

Chris would love to laugh at me now.

I squeeze my eyes shut, refusing to think about him. If I do, I'll turn back. So I force myself to relax.

After a while I doze off. I sleep until sunrise, waking up to find everything covered with a thin sheet of frost. I sit up, wiggling my stiff fingers.

I eat a quick meal of dried meat and crackers, then get moving. I try to stay out of the foliage as much as possible, knowing that animals are at their most active stage during the early hours of morning. Of course, I always assumed that most creatures went into hibernation during the winter, but why risk walking into a snoozing bear if I don't have to?

Another reason I miss Chris. He makes a great decoy.

At around ten o'clock, I arrive at the entrance to Sequoia National Park. The road widens into five lanes, all separated with yellow lines. There are two streamlined check-in stations in the middle of the road, marked with the National Forestry insignia. But that's not what draws my attention: on the right-hand side of the road, there is a redwood tree as big as a building. The trunk is bigger than ten SUVs, towering above the highway with gigantic branches.

It's stunning.

I smile, remembering driving through here with Dad last year on summer vacation. We would always come to the cabin and hang out for a week or two, but everything was different, then. Obviously. There were cars and tourists at the entrance to the park. It was exciting.

Now it's lonely. And it makes me think. Maybe the forest, the trees, everything out here, is happy that there aren't any cars plowing through the roads, spitting diesel fumes. Without people around, there won't be any idiots to leave empty beer bottles behind at campgrounds or throw dirty napkins out the window for the wildlife to ingest.

I sigh.

I guess if there's a bright side to this situation, this would be it.

About an hour later, I pause at the corner of curve number five-thousand, sniffing the air. I smell...smoke. It's a light, woodsy scent that reminds me of burning pine needles. I tighten my hands around the straps of my backpack, nervous. Where's there's smoke, there's usually people. Fire doesn't just *happen* unless lightning and a tall tree is involved.

I walk right off the road, putting a few feet between me and the open space of the highway. As I progress, the smell becomes stronger.

And then I hear laughter.

Every muscle in my body freezes. Why?

A) If there are people here, there's a good chance that they're not friendly because B) they're probably Omega soldiers looking for someone to harass.

I drop to my stomach, crawling forward on hands and knees through the brush. The laughter gets louder, and there's definitely a girl's voice mixed in with it. I get a nose full of bear clover as I keep my body perfectly still, glued to the scene in front of me.

Across the road, past a clump of fern, is a campfire. Tendrils of smoke rise up and drift toward me. Three people are gathered around it: A girl with a blonde ponytail, and two guys, one with dark hair and another that looks like he could be the girl's brother.

They don't look like Omega hacks to me. Friend or foe?

I rest my chin in my hands, thinking back to the abandoned baby carrier on the side of the road when Chris and I first escaped LA.

There are a lot of crazies in the world, I think. *I'd better play it safe.*

But I'm afraid that if I move backwards, they'll see me. It's probably a miracle that they didn't hear my footsteps on the pavement. So I stay here, trying to think of a way to get around these people without being seen and without getting lost.

What would Chris do?

He'd avoid them altogether.

One of the boys at the campfire, the one with the blonde hair, stands up and stretches. He says something to his friends and disappears into the bushes. I assume he's going to collect firewood.

I slowly lift myself up enough to wiggle backwards, trying to make the least amount of noise as possible. I'll just go back the way I came and make a wide detour past their campfire, hope we don't run into each other again, and be on my merry way.

Problem solved.

As I retreat, the soft voices of the strangers fade. My heartbeat slows. If I can't hear them, they can't hear me. Right? I sit up with my legs tucked under me. Crisis averted.

"Gotcha!"

A strangled scream dies in my throat as someone grabs the collar of my coat and yanks me upright. I see a flash of blonde hair and green eyes, and for a split second I think it's Chris. Relief floods through me, but it doesn't last, as usual. It's not Chris. It's the blonde boy from the campfire.

He's got a boyish face – maybe fifteen years old – but he's almost three times as big as me. "I got her!" he yells across the road. His voice is *way* too loud. Is he stupid? "She was *spying* on us."

He's got one hand around my neck, and the other is wound around the belt of my pants. I'm facing away from him, so I can't turn around and claw his eyes out with my fingers.

"Let go!" I say, choking.

"What do you want?"

The blonde walks toward me, trailed by the kid with dark hair. They're all high school age, no older then the guy currently using me as a stress ball. "Um...choking...can't...talk," I sputter, feeling my cheeks turn red.

"Drop her," Blondie says.

The guy I privately dub *Choker* lets go. I stagger forward, gasping for air. "Geez. Thanks a lot," I spit, breathing hard. "Are you insane?"

The dark-haired one looks down at me.

"Why were you watching us?"

"Why were you watching *me*?"

"I asked first."

"You almost choked me to death." I shoot Choker a glare.

The three exchange puzzled glances. Maybe they were expecting me to pick them off one by one with a sniper rifle while I hid in the bear clover. A side effect of watching too many teen television shows.

"Come on. Back to the fire," Blondie commands, her arms crossed. "Bring her."

Choker and the dark-haired one each take an arm, hauling me across the road. I should make a run for it, but hey. Maybe they've got food or coffee they're just dying to share with me.

"Sit."

Blondie plops down on a log, her legs crossed. The boys stay on each side of me, and then Choker leans behind Blondie's log and grabs a hunting rifle. He keeps it trained at my head, his finger *on* the trigger.

I suddenly feel very uncool about all of this.

"What's up with you guys?" I ask. "I'm just hiking. That's all."

"Right," Blondie laughs, and it annoys me. It's a cruel laugh. "You were just *hiking*? Nobody's just "hiking" up here anymore. We're not that stupid."

"That's a debatable point," I say.

Blondie glares.

"Were you planning on stealing our food?" she asks, her lip curling. "Maybe killing us in our sleep and taking our supplies?"

"Um…" I roll my eyes. "Yeah. That was definitely my plan. You got me."

The dark-haired boy opens his mouth to speak for the first time.

"Maybe she's okay," he says softly. "Maybe she's telling the truth."

"No." Blondie's hands tighten into fists. "I'm keeping my eye on her. We *all* are."

I sigh dramatically.

"So now what? You're going to tie me up and cook me for dinner?" I ask. "I don't have a lot of meat on my bones."

Blondie kicks me in the shins.

It doesn't hurt. But it *does* tick me off.

"Knock it off," I say, kicking back.

She cries out, completely falsifying the amount of pain she feels.

"See?" she gasps. "She's dangerous. Take her stuff. Tie her up. We can't trust her."

"Ditto, darling," I say, relaxing into my predicament.

Even though Choker is aiming the rifle at my head, and even though his finger is on the trigger (didn't anybody teach him firearms safety techniques?), his hands are shaking. He doesn't look like he wants to kill me. He looks like he's afraid of me.

Good.

The dark-haired boy moves quickly, pulling a pair of plastic ties from his daypack. He cinches up my wrists tightly, drawing blood. He doesn't apologize. He only stares straight ahead, his eyes empty, his face emotionless.

"You move, redhead, and he'll kill you," Blondie warns, crouching over the fire. "Got that?"

"Right," I reply. I don't believe them. "Is there a reason you're making a campfire in the middle of the day, by the way?"

"None of your business," Choker growls, sitting down. He keeps the rifle in his lap, watching me closely.

"Look," I say, "here's the thing: I need to find my dad. We got separated and I'm going to be seriously late if you keep me here."

"She's lying," Blondie replies, spitting out the words. "Why would she be spying on us if she was really trying to find her dad?"

"Oh, I don't know," I say. "Maybe because the world has gone insane and I don't know who I can trust?" I look around at them. "Exhibit A."

Blondie stalks across the small camp area and smacks me across the face. I blink back tears from the sting of the blow.

Now I'm mad.

"That was ladylike," I remark. "Thanks for that."

She turns around and begins rifling through my backpack.

"Leave my stuff alone," I say.

"Shut up." She pulls out some of my food, then the knife Jeff gave me for Christmas. "Junk."

She shoves it back inside and approaches me again. She zips my coat open, patting me down.

"This is getting weird," I say, shoving away from her. "Stop."

"Hold *still*, Ginger," she sneers.

She searches my pockets, discarding my waterproof matches, tissue, and rubber bands. Her fingers pause at my neck, where the gold chain that Chris gave me catches the sunlight.

"Don't even think about it," I warn.

She smiles nastily and snaps the gold chain off my neck. She holds it in front of her face, the tiny shield with Chris's name in silver glimmering against the gold.

"Pretty," she says. "Thanks."

"Give that back," I say, and this time, I'm done being nice. *Chris* gave that to me. How dare she? "Don't make me remove that from your neck."

Blondie drops the snapped chain into her pocket.

"We can use this later."

Choker looks a little disturbed but the dark-haired boy – I'm calling him *Spot*, now – doesn't look like he cares.

"Give. It. Back," I say.

"Come and get it," Blondie replies, grinning.

I shift my position, but as soon as I move, Choker aims the rifle at my head again. "Don't move," he warns. Spot also places his hand on my forearm.

This is going to be a long day.

Blondie pats her pocket and proceeds to pull supplies out of their own packs. They've got quite a bit of food and first aid stuff. Sleeping bags, even. Maybe they were camping out here when the pulse hit.

I also notice a NYC keychain on one of the backpacks.

"You're from New York," I say.

186

Blondie looks up at me, startled.

"How did you know that?" she demands.

"I read a lot of Sherlock Holmes books when I was a kid," I reply.

"What does *that* mean?"

"Forget it," I sigh. "Look. Give me my stuff and I'll get out of here."

"No." Blondie sets to work making some sort of stew. "I don't trust you."

"If this is how you treat all the people you meet, you're never going to be very popular," I comment.

She curses me. Explicitly.

I ignore the rude remark and look away. I sit on the ground and lean against the log, tired. Blondie and her cohorts treat themselves to a meal when, but they never invite me to join the feast. After an hour or so, my lips are chapped and I'm dying for water.

"I need water," I say.

"Suck it up and deal with it," Blondie snaps.

I am *so* going to stick her head in a hole.

Besides her outright meanness, Blondie – along with her male companions – are stupid. They're camping during daylight hours. Their campfire is sending a beacon of smoke into the air. And they're *loud.*

Survival skills? None.

Halfway through the day, Choker decides to engage in target practice with his rifle. He makes two mistakes: One, he's wasting precious ammunition. Two, he's making an enormous amount of noise and practically setting up a giant neon arrow over our heads that says, OMEGA: COME FIND US.

Thankfully, the day passes without incident. Nighttime comes and Blondie keeps the fire going at a pretty big blaze. It's too big. Too noticeable. A lot of smoke.

"Where are you guys headed?" I ask. The three of them are bent over their dinner – a dinner no one shared with me yet again.

My stomach growls.

"We're not headed anywhere," Choker replies. "We're just wandering."

"Shut *up*," Blondie snaps, slapping his knee. "Don't tell her anything."

"That's too bad," I shrug. "Because I'm familiar with these mountains, and you're not...and we could probably help each other if you'd just *let* me."

Blondie doesn't respond, but I can see the wheels turning in her head. Choker almost smiles. Spot...well, he just gazes into the fire, like he's been doing all day.

I wonder what these messed-up kids have been through.

"Look, you're making some big mistakes here," I say. "First of all, you shouldn't have a fire this big, this close to the road, or in the same place for so long. Omega troops could see it and find you. Who knows how widespread their forces are? You need to quit wasting ammo and firing shots when you don't need to. Save the bullets for the bad guys."

Choker stares at me, an expression of amazement on his face.

"You know a lot about survival?" he asks.

"Enough."

"How much?' Spot says suddenly, his brown eyes searching my face.

"Come on, guys," Blondie whines. "Are you seriously going to believe this chick?"

"Don't get jealous, city girl," I reply, my tone sharp. "I don't think growing up in New York taught *you* very much about survival."

She frowns, looking away.

Yeah, that's what I thought.

"Bree, maybe we should listen to her," Spot says, using Blondie's real name for the first time. "Look at her. She looks like she knows what she's doing."

"No *freaking* way," Blondie snarls, and when she turns back to us, tears are shining in her eyes. "I know what I'm doing. We don't need anybody's help. *Especially* some girl's."

"You lost your parents, didn't you?" I say, realization dawning. "I'm sorry."

Choker looks down. Blondie glares at me, her lower lip trembling.

"None of your business," she replies, standing up. "I'm getting some more firewood."

As she crashes through the undergrowth, Spot looks at me from his place beside me. "Yes," he whispers. "We lost them."

"When did this happen?" I ask, the sadness in his expression deep. Piercing.

"The day everything died," he said. "They were driving the car in front of us. Went off a cliff."

A lead weight settles in the bottom of my gut. Saddened, I say the only thing I can say. "I'm sorry."

I really am.

The next day is exactly the same. Blondie – Bree – is rude and Choker guards me like a faithful St. Bernard. Spot hangs out around the fire, doing nothing. The boy is *depressed*.

I'm forced to sit near the eternal campfire. They never offer to cut the tight plastic cord around my wrists. Choker gives me limited food and water when Blondie's not around. It's enough to keep me alive.

I can't really run off without my stuff, so I wait for an opportunity to get my gear and Chris's graduation chain.

"Aren't you guys ever going to *move*?" I say.

While my sympathy for their loss is real, I can't believe that anybody would be stupid enough to camp out next to the road. Sheer dumb luck is the only reason they haven't been found by unsavory characters.

"We're fine right here," Blondie replies.

"It's winter. You can't go very long without running into a storm."

"Mind your own business."

"I will when you tell me what you plan on doing with me," I say. "Because I can't just sit here forever, and since you won't take my advice, I'm thinking that I want to get out of here before Omega swoops in and kills us all."

"Omega?" she replies. "What's *Omega*?"

I blink a few times before the truth hits me: how would they know about Omega? They've been hiding in the mountains, isolated from the outside world since the EMP hit.

"Omega is behind the EMP," I explain. "They're invading the state – maybe the whole country. Everything's down and they're rounding up civilians, sending them to concentration camps."

Blondie exhales.

"Riiiight," she drawls. "Sure."

I lower my head.

Why do I even try?

I really need to get out of here. But I have to patient. My best bet at escape will be during the night. At least two of them will be asleep, while one of the boys stays up to keep guard.

I'll improvise.

Until then, it's boredom central. I take advantage of the opportunity to rest. I anxiously scan the skies when I'm awake, noting the approach of heavy, dark clouds over the higher mountains. A storm is coming.

When I mention the storm, they don't show signs of concern. I eventually come to the conclusion that all three of them are in a state of denial over their situation. They don't intend to break a sweat to survive.

Screw *that* approach. I want to live.

When it gets dark, Blondie and Spot fall asleep while Choker stays up to watch me. I lean against the backpack, puzzling out how I'm going to escape. I could ask to go to the bathroom and sneak off into the night...but I don't want to leave without Chris's chain and my backpack.

So what's my game plan?

The distant roll of thunder over Kings Canyon startles me. Great. There's probably a flood washing down the canyons at this very moment. But will they care? No.

I sit upright, listening to the thunder roll again. And again.

And...

I stop moving, a chill crawling up my spine. The thunder is steady, getting louder. Getting...closer. Oh, my God. I stand up, more noise joining the first chorus of what I thought was thunder.

Because it's not.

It's the engine of a truck.

Choker stands up across the campfire, watching my movements.

"Don't try to make a run for it," he says, yawning.

"Wake up, Bree!" I ignore Choker and kick her foot.

"What the-?" she begins, anger flashing across her face. "What are you *doing*, Ginger?"

"Trucks. Coming this way," I warn. "Quick. Put out the fire. Get your gun loaded. We need to move *now*."

"Are you kidding?" Blondie rolls out of her sleeping bag, excitement written across her features. "Trucks mean people and people mean help. We can go home!"

"Are you crazy?" I hiss. "They'll kill us. No civilians' cars are working right now. Omega vehicles are, but that's it. Listen to me. You stay here and you're dead."

"Shut her up," Blondie commands, looking absolutely livid. "We're going home, boys."

"No you're not!" I press. "Don't be stupid! You're going to get everyone killed!"

Blondie pulls her hood across her face.

And just like that, she trots off into the darkness, following the sound of the trucks.

Dear Lord, she's lost her mind.

"Stop her!" I tell the boys.

They just look at me with blank expressions.

192

"We *do* need help," Choker shrugs.

I narrow my eyes.

"Yeah. And it's not going to be from me."

I slam my boot right between his legs, putting all my force into it. Choker cries out, dropping the rifle to the ground. Spot jumps out of his sleeping bag, looking momentarily terrified before he rushes toward me, trying to bring me down.

No. I'm not in the mood.

My wrists are still tied together, so I slam both my fists across his face in what's possibly the most unorthodox punch in the history of self-defense. Spot stumbles backwards as I deliver a beautiful roundhouse kick to make my point. He crashes down, clutching his head and moaning.

Not bad, Cassidy.

I reach down, grab the rifle, and aim it at Choker.

"Open my backpack and get my knife out," I say. "And do it quickly."

Choker crawls across the dirt, dragging my backpack out from behind the log. He fumbles around before pulling out the knife.

"Give it to Spot," I command.

Choker looks at me, confused, and I realize that I'm using their nicknames aloud. Oh, well.

Choker tosses the knife to Spot, who stares at is as it lies on the ground. In the not-so-far-off distance, the sound of multiple trucks screeches loudly against the night sky. Do I hear voices, too?

"Pick up the knife," I say, "and cut these plastic ties off my wrist."

I walk over to Spot, kneel, and keep my rifle trained on Choker's head for the maximum effect. Spot, dizzy and disoriented from the two smacks I gave him, obeys without thinking. He picks up Jeff's knife and cuts through the binds.

I exhale, loving the freedom of movement.

"Stay where you are, big guy," I tell Choker.

I grab my backpack, strap the knife to my belt, and keep the rifle within easy reach. "I would suggest that you run," I advise, "because trust me when I say that what's coming isn't..." I trail off as Blondie's piercing scream rips through the air.

Without a second glance at Choker and Spot, I sprint forward into the darkness, wishing to God those boys would kill the light from the fire.

On second thought, I hope they just run.

Blondie screams again. There are voices. It sounds like some of the trucks' engines have been cut, which means whoever's coming is getting out of their vehicles. "Bree!" I shout, desperate.

Why do I care what happens to her?

"Bree, answer me!"

A gunshot breaks the monotone of the truck engines. Dread hits me like a punch in the chest as I run in the direction where the gunshot was fired. I can't see, but I can hear. "Bree? Bree!"

I stop and listen, leaning against a tree.

And then,

"Ginger?"

It's faint, but it's her voice. I scramble toward it, dropping to my hands and knees. I crawl through the mud and leaves until I touch warm flesh, Bree's hand.

"Bree," I say, leaning over her. I can't see. "Are you...?"

I run my hands up her body, trying to find her face, but I stop.

There's hot, sticky blood on her abdomen. "Oh, my God, Bree…" I breathe, choking on a gag. "I'm so sorry…"

Her breathing is heavy as her hand gropes for my face. When she finally finds it, she pulls my head forward and whispers, "I'm sorry, Ginger."

She drops something into my lap. Her hand falls away from my face, hitting the ground with a soft thud. I push my fist against my mouth to keep from crying out, checking her wrist, her chest, and her neck for any sign of a pulse.

But there's nothing.

She's dead.

Trembling , I reach into my lap. My fingers brush cool metal.

Chris's gold chain.

I bite my lip, stuffing it into my pocket. I need to run. I need to move. Now. But I can't leave her here like this. What kind of a person would I be?

"Hey, stop!"

It's a man's voice. It doesn't seem like it's directed at me. There are flashlights about fifty feet away from me, combing through the woods. From here I can see dark shadows moving around the orange light of the campfire.

"Run, boys," I murmur, leaning forward.

I compulsively press a kiss to Blondie's – *Bree's* – forehead and climb to my feet, feeling like I'm moving through a dream. I just held a girl's hand as she *died*. Am I really doing this?

"I'm so sorry," I whisper again.

Another gunshot. A scream.

Choker? Spot?

I have to go. I turn and break into a run, streaking through the dark forest, occasionally stumbling over roots and stones. Another scream. I slow to a halt. What am I doing? I can't leave those dumb kids to fend for themselves.

Against my better judgment, I take the rifle in my hands and feel for the safety switch. It's off. I make sure it's loaded and begin running again...in the opposite direction. As I near the campfire, I hear the pleading, pathetic voices of Spot and Choker. I creep closer, staying out of the way of flashlight beams.

I inhale.

There are only *two* Omega soldiers. One's got a gun, while the other holds a flashlight. Spot and Choker are on their knees with their hands behind their heads. I can hear more voices in the distance, which means this party's about to be crashed by more animals.

I drop to my stomach, holding the gun close to my cheek, the stock steady against my shoulder. I look through the sight, taking a deep breath. I used to play Airsoft with my cousin when I was younger, and it wasn't much different than this.

Omega guard Number One has his gun cocked and aimed at Choker's head. Anger tears through my body, making me hot. I've still got Bree's blood on my left hand, reminding me just how capable these guys are of taking a human life.

I aim my rifle, check the sight one more time, and pray.

Then I squeeze the trigger.

The Omega guard with the gun screams, and both of the guys drop to the ground for cover. I fire a few rounds into the dirt, scaring the crap out of both of them. They drag themselves away from the fire, and in the process, Choker and Spot hunker down with their hands behind their necks.

As the troopers run, I realize something:

I have the perfect opportunity to kill both of them.

And why shouldn't I? Stupid, pathetic bullies who enjoy killing innocent men, women and children don't deserve any mercy from me.

But I'm not like them, am I?

I don't kill people.

It's not my job to decide who lives or dies. I guess that's what sets me apart from the enemy in this game of survival.

This State of Emergency.

So I fire another shot, the two Omega soldiers checking out and making a mad dash through the darkness, calling for backup. I stand and run through the bushes, wired with adrenaline.

"Get up!"

I break into camp. Choker and Spot are staring at me with wide eyes, both covered with tears. "Listen to me," I say, grabbing Spot by the collar. "Run. Run as fast as you can, as far as you can. Get your gear and go. Do you understand me?"

He nods weakly, moaning something about Bree.

I don't want to tell him that his sister's dead, so I don't. He's probably figured it out already, judging by the blood I just smeared across his shirt. "Just run," I say again.

I toss the rifle into his arms.

He holds it awkwardly, frozen. I turn away from the fire and make my way back into the woods, stopping only when Spot says,

"Thank you." I cast him a final glance. He looks confused. "And my name's Jack. This is Peter."

I almost smile, but I'm too shell-shocked.

"Cassidy," I whisper.

And then I run.

At dawn, I stop.

I kneel at the base of a redwood tree, gasping for breath I have lost all sense of direction running through the darkness. I pushed hard, and I pushed fast. Away from the trucks and the shots.

And now I'm lost.

I lay my head against the tree, pulling a canteen out of my backpack with shaky hands. I'm not cold, I'm exhausted. Shocked.

I close my eyes.

When I open them again, it's late morning. I surmise that I must have slept for three hours. Chilled, I force myself to eat jerky and crackers. I have no appetite, but starvation isn't going to earn me bonus points in the *staying alive* category, so I choke it down anyway.

When I have my strength back, I get up and start walking. North? South? Which way am I going? I can barely see the sky through the trees. I can't find the sun. On top of that, an icy wind cuts across the side of the mountain, frigid and piercing.

What happened to Peter and Jack? Are they still alive? How many children are in the same position? How many kids have been orphaned and hunted down for committing the simple crime of existing? And what about Bree? I look down at my left hand. Under the glove, I wasn't able to get all the blood off my hand.

It makes me sick to look at it.

So I don't.

Instead I continue to wander the forest, going nowhere. Completely lost. No matter which way I go, I can't seem to find the main highway again. Every stick and patch of weeds looks exactly the same. I actually get dizzy from walking in so many circles. The forest closes in on me, eating me alive. There's no escape.

Okay. Now what? What am I supposed to do when I get lost?

1.   Hug a tree.

2.   Blow a whistle, if you have it.

3.   Avoid wild animals.

4.   DON'T PANIC.

5.   Stay in the same place until someone finds you.

There's one problem. Omega is the *someone* who might be looking for me, and I don't want to be found. There will be no rescue helicopters or forest rangers combing the forest for my whereabouts. I am alone.

I'm so screwed.

When Dad and I drove up to the cabin every summer, we followed the main highway, veering onto a lesser known mountain road until we blew it off altogether, hitting a dirt trail that climbed the side of the mountain. It was virtually invisible to the outside world, but I knew the route by heart.

Now? Not so much.

I'm lost. I deviated from the route. I'm paying the price.

Calm down, I tell myself. *Just find the road and you'll be okay.*

I press ahead with confidence that I don't have. I walk in a straight line for two hours, heading uphill. The side of the mountain is so steep that I have to dig my feet into the mountain at a parallel angle, climbing on hands and knees. By the time I reach the top, my muscles are on fire and I'm breathing hard.

Making matters even more fantastic, I'm left to look at yet another huge mountain, more woods, more rocks, more fern. But no highway. I take a breather and skirt the bottom of the next incline, following a battered animal trail probably used by deer. I end up looking at a small boulder that looks suspiciously like one I passed a couple of hours ago.

I bend to inspect the dirt, looking at the indents in the soft mud around the rock. There are footprints. *Boot* prints if I'm going to be technical. I study them closely, wondering if they're mine. Because if they are, I'm even more lost than I thought.

I compare the bottom of my shoe to the print in the mud, but it's so faint that I can't really tell. I hold my boot right over the print to compare sizes, hovering in place like a butterfly.

The shoe is a *lot* bigger than mine.

I pull my leg back, spooked. The footprint is fresh. It hasn't even dried around the edges yet.

I look around the woods, every shadow seeming bigger and darker than it did a moment ago. Am I being followed? Tracked? Impossible. I would have heard pursuers.

Wouldn't I?

I cinch my backpack and decide to solve this navigational issue once and for all. If someone is following me, I don't want to find out who it is. I don't have any weapons besides the knife Jeff gave me.

What I know:

I'm lost. But I also know that the highway was running south to north when I was forced to make an unexpected pit stop by Bree and her brothers. If I travel in the same direction again, I'll eventually run into the highway, right? I can't be more than ten miles away from the place I left Jack and Peter. The road has to be nearby.

I walk in a quick circle, observing the trees. I find a cedar tree with low-hanging branches and pull myself up. I keep climbing, scraping my palms against the sharp bark. I drop my backpack to the ground. It's too hard to maneuver the tree with a pack hanging off my shoulders.

I climb higher and higher, until vertigo kicks in and glues my arms to the tree trunk. I'm up *really* high. So high that I can actually feel the tree swaying with every gust of wind.

I maintain a firm grip, moving my gaze across the horizon. I can see over the bulk of the canopy of trees. The sky is dark. Snow is coming.

I can't see the highway, of course, but I *can* see the sun. It's close to noon, which makes it easy for me to tell which way east is. Once I figure that out, I'm able to find west, south and north. Awesome.

I shimmy down, slipping a few times and catching myself on another branch. When I get to the bottom, I jump from the low branch and land in a crouch.

"Now we're in business," I say out loud, grabbing my pack.

Crunch.

I stop. I'm so tired of being ambushed. Suspicious sounds are starting to get annoying. I look around, see nobody, and start walking north. All I have to do is keep this course and I'll eventually run into the highway – *some* highway – again. From there I can find the cabin.

Snap!

Okay. That was *definitely* something with weight behind it. More than a squirrel, anyway. I whirl around, taking a step backwards. Someone's out there.

Down the hill, a dark figure is creeping up the trail behind me. I stand there, motionless, staring at the person. Whoever it is, he's wearing black.

He could be anybody...a mercenary *or* Omega soldier.

I don't stop to wave hello. I just run. Which, of course, means I've got to climb the next hill I've been avoiding. It cuts up at an angle, nearly a sheer cliff.

I get to work, digging my feet into the dirt and using trees, roots, rocks and the occasional sprout to pull myself up. And then I do something I regret: I look behind me. The black shirted figure is gaining. He's not keeping his presence a secret, and it makes me wonder if he's alone. Are there more of them back there? Did they figure out that it was me who fired rounds at the guys trying to kill Peter and Jack?

Don't think, climb!

I climb until every muscle in my body simply refuses to move anymore. I slip on a bed of pine needles and slide on my hip down the hill. A twenty-foot drop. I push myself back up, panicked.

Come on, girl. Stay calm.

"Cassidy!"

I stumble, confused.

Peter?

Jack?

I slip again, catching my breath. The guy has a black bandana tied around his hooded head, decked out in black combat pants and boots. He's got a heavy coat on, a rifle slung over his back.

"Chris?" I stutter.

He pulls his hood off, revealing a face I recognize – but it's smeared with black paint and dirt. It *is* Chris, right?

"Who the hell else would it be?" He climbs the last few feet separating us and yanks me to my feet, throwing me against his chest. I grab his shoulders as he presses a fierce kiss to my lips. I fold my arms around his neck, threading my fingers through his hair. He pulls away suddenly and glares, hands gripping my hips so hard I think he's leaving bruises.

"What were you thinking?" he demands.

I touch my mouth, black camo paint sticking to my fingers. I stare up at him, his beautiful green eyes flashing with anger.

"I had to go, Chris," I say. "You know that."

"I thought you were *dead*," he says, holding me with one arm, his other hand cupping my cheek. His hands are wrapped up with strips of cloth.

"I can take care of myself."

But while I'm talking, all I can think is:

Chris is here. With me.

I am flooded with complete, utter relief.

"I found a dead body a few miles back," Chris says. "Omega was out in full force in the lower part of the mountains. They're searching for campers in the hills. I thought maybe you were caught in the crossfire."

I pale, realizing he must have found Bree.

"Did you find anybody else?" I whisper.

"No. Why?"

I shake my head.

"I was there," I say.

Chris squeezes me tighter.

"I've been tracking you since you left," he tells me, his thumb trailing down the side of my neck. "Why would you do that to me?"

"Do what?"

"Leave without saying goodbye."

I sigh.

"I don't know." And it's an honest answer. "I guess I didn't want to make you choose between me and your family."

He looks shocked and then kisses me slowly, sending a shiver down my spine. Everything around us dissolves – the cold weather, the trees, the dirt. It's just the two of us, and the only thing that matters is that he's holding me, and I feel safe.

Completely safe.

"I think we already had this discussion," he says, his voice soft. "You *are* a part of the family, now. So you should start acting like it."

I lower my eyes.

"I'm sorry," I answer. "I just had to go before I lost my nerve."

My lower lip wobbles, tears threatening to spill down my cheeks. "Chris, the body you found," I say. "I was with that girl when she died."

His gaze narrows and a muscle ticks in his jaw.

"And you're lost," he states. "Tell me what happened."

I nod, sitting down. Chris keeps his arms around me as we lean against the base of a tree. I snuggle into his warmth.

I'm safe. I'm safe.

I give him the whole story, leaving out no detail, and by the time I end my sad tale, I'm crying gently.

"I didn't even know Bree," I choke. "But nobody deserves to die like that."

"No, they don't," Chris agrees, drawing his hand down my arm. Soothing me. "It wasn't your fault."

"I tried to tell them," I say. "But they wouldn't listen."

"Hey, look at me," Chris says, tilting my chin up. "You went back and saved those kids' lives when you could have kept running. You didn't do anything wrong. Forget about this, okay?"

I nod slightly. He kisses the tip of my nose.

"You feel like moving?" he asks.

"Where are we going?"

"To your cabin. Or has there been a change of plans?"

I blink a few times. It honestly hadn't crossed my mind that Chris was going to help me find my father. I thought he would come here and then drag me back to his home.

"You're coming with me?" I exclaim, a smile creeping across my face.

"Cassidy," he whispers, taking my hands in his, "where else would I be?"

Chapter Thirteen

There's something about the forest that invigorates your senses. It's the kind of feeling you can't get if you're strolling down a sidewalk in the city. It's a feeling of absolute freedom. You feel that, despite the urbanization and craziness in the rest of the world, the forest is a sacred place. A refuge of solace.

Chris is able to find the highway again. He's a tracker, a hunter.

A SEAL. His skills are flawless.

I ask him why he didn't take the Hummer we stole from Omega in the valley to find me, and he says he wouldn't have been able to track me in a car.

I don't bother to ask *how* he tracked me.

As we get higher, it gets colder. The air becomes drier and I swear the elevation change makes me hungrier. Note: Hungrier than *usual*. Chris has more supplies in his backpack, which means my chances of starving to death are a little smaller than they were when I was on my own.

There are still no cars or signs of humans. Neither is there any sign of an evacuation. It's possible that the limited population here is still in the dark about the Omega invasion – isolated and with no contact with outside world...how would they know what's happened?

We cover about four miles. I can't go any farther. I'm exhausted. We find a place to camp off the road. I curl up in a tight ball next to Chris. He keeps me warm, and his presence is comforting.

"Have you ever been camping before?" I ask.

"Yeah." Chris shifts his arm underneath me, pulling me closer. No complaint here. "You?"

"No."

"Seriously?"

"Seriously."

"But you and your dad have a cabin up here," he says. "Haven't you ever been up here before? To a campground?"

"Believe me, our cabin is pretty much the same thing as camping," I reply, smiling. "The only difference is the roof and the mattresses. Other than that, it's like sleeping outside."

Silence.

"What are you going to do if he's not there, Cassidy?" he finally asks. I finger the zipper on his jacket, listening to the calm beat of his heart against my ear.

"I don't know," I reply. "I don't want to think about it."

"You need to. We're lucky that it's a dry season," he says. "But all it takes is one big storm to trap you somewhere. You need to decide if you're going to stay there and wait for him, or if you'd come back to the house with me if he wasn't there."

"Can't I just decide when we get there?" I ask.

He doesn't answer, which is his way of saying, "You can, but you shouldn't."

So that's what I decide to do. If my father isn't there, I'll return home with Chris. I'll have no choice. Survival is survival, and neither of us wants to get stuck in the higher mountains alone.

I'll have to move on.

"Hey, don't worry about it," Chris says, rubbing my arm. "It'll work out."

"Yeah," I reply, unconvinced. "Sure it will."

We sleep well until twilight. Prime bear-roaming time. I awake severely chilled. Chris, however, seems unaffected.

That's a Navy SEAL for you. Oblivious to cold temperatures.

We eat a quick breakfast, and then we're on our way.

The highway becomes windier the higher we climb. Chris says it smells like a winter storm, and the sky is now covered with thick, dark clouds.

And I didn't even bring an umbrella.

Every once in a while the road will peek out of the trees and give us a great view of the landscape below. Chris hikes to the side of the road and places his boot on the guardrail. I, on the other hand, don't feel the need to get *that* close to the cliffs.

I observe from a safer distance.

My second day with Chris finds us about twelve miles closer to my cabin, and a lot deeper into the forest. There are still no signs of human activity, which is fine with me.

No people? No Omega.

At the beginning of the third day, I begin to get concerned about the thick cloud cover.

"Look at those clouds," I say, tilting my head up. The sky is covered with dark, fat clouds. "Do you think they're trouble?"

"They're full of snow," Chris replies. "How far is your cabin from here?"

"I'd say about two days. We're deep into the woods."

He grunts. I fall into step beside him, pulling my hat over my ears. "Are we heading into this snowstorm?" I ask.

"It's likely," he replies.

"Will it hit before we get to the cabin?"

"We'll be okay," he replies, "as long as we keep moving."

He doesn't give voice to the fact that there is *definitely* a chance that we will get caught in the storm before we reach the cabin. This frightens me. I've never been in a snowstorm before, but I know that they can be deadly.

"Are you *sure* we'll be okay?" I ask.

"Yes, Cassidy," Chris replies, a shadow of a smile on lips. "It's just snow, not a nuclear explosion."

He slips his arm around my waist and kisses my cheek. I can't help but brighten a bit. By the time we stop for the night, the temperature has dropped substantially. It's a biting, driving cold. The kind that makes your bones hurt.

"Don't talk yourself into freezing to death," Chris says matter-of-factly.

I pull a portable gas camping stove out of Chris's backpack.

"Stop shivering," he continues, watching my movements. "You're going to make yourself colder if you give into it. Think warm thoughts."

"I *am!*"

Chris studies my face for a long time. I place a tin pot of water on the stove. Once the water is hot, I remove a teabag from the backpack and drop it in the pot.

"What are you staring at?" I finally say, waiting for the tea to steep.

"Your lips are turning blue," he replies.

"No, they're not," I deny. But he's right. They hurt.

Chris rolls his eyes and moves next to me. He spreads his legs apart and wraps his arms around my waist, pulling me back against his chest. Then he boxes me in with all his limbs and begins rubbing my arms.

I say, "I think my tea is ready."

I take a sip of the hot liquid. Yes. It's ready. I hand a tin cup to Chris and pour him some tea. He takes a drink before giving it back to me. The tea doesn't have any nutritional value, but the warmth is comforting.

"I hope we don't freeze to death," I comment.

"We won't."

"It could happen. People die in the mountains all the time."

"People who don't know what they're doing."

I purse my blue lips.

"Yeah...?"

Chris chuckles low in his chest, placing his lips close to my ear.

"I won't let you freeze to death, little girl," he says. "Relax."

I try. We roll to our sides, pressed together to stay warm.

It takes me a long time to go to sleep. I'm too tense. Too cold. But I doze off eventually. At that point Chris shakes me awake.

"Cassidy, wake up," he says, shaking my shoulders. "It's snowing."

I struggle to pull myself upright, unable to feel my hands. My face is totally frozen. I can barely move my mouth. When I open my eyes all I can see is a fine layer of white covering everything: the ground, the trees, our backpacks. Me.

It's snowing.

"Um..." I can't think of anything else to say, mainly because I can't arrange my mouth to *say* it. "I'm frozen."

210

"I can see that." Chris hooks his arms underneath my shoulders and pulls me upright. I'm stiff.

"Oh, my God," I say. "I *did* freeze during the night."

"You're just a little chilled," Chris replies. "As soon as we get moving you'll be fine."

"I can't feel my feet," I complain.

"You'll warm up as soon as we start moving."

We move quickly. The biting temperature is an excellent motivation to avoid lingering in any one place too long. I throw on my backpack and trudge up a slippery bank of pine needles to the highway.

We walk all day through the snow, freezing our butts off until nightfall, where we make camp again. We don't sleep long because it's too cold – even Chris doesn't like to stop moving.

We make another six or seven miles by mid-afternoon before coming to a campground. Snow is covering the roads, nearly six inches deep. Every time I exhale, my breath makes white puffs in the air.

You *know* it's cold when you can see your own breath.

The campground is nestled in the big trees off to the left. On the right is a tourist center. There's a grocery store and a public restroom facility. There's even a restaurant. Dull lights are flickering in the windows. The building is painted a rusty brown color.

"Do you see what I see?" I wonder.

"Yeah," Chris replies. "It looks like they're open for business."

"No way. Out in the middle of nowhere?"

"It looks like it."

"It looks warm. Should we check it out?"

Chris tilts his head.

"Yeah. We don't have any other options right now."

"What if Omega is in there?"

"Then we're in trouble."

We go ahead anyway. Not because we're stupid or reckless. But because this winter storm will be the death of us – or at least *me* – if we don't find shelter soon. It's worth the risk.

We make our way through the snow, leaving footprints behind us. By the time we get close enough to the restaurant, I see a sign that says: **Survivors Welcome**.

I glance at Chris.

"Score," I say.

We pick up the pace and make it across the empty parking lot. Quads and old motorcycles are parked out front. We ascend creaky steps, open a thick door and step inside.

The first thing that hits me is the fantastic, mouth-watering scent.

And then I take in the building.

It's basically an oversized cabin with hardwood floors, tables and chairs. Lamps hang from the ceiling, lighting the interior. There are also quite a few people. Most of them look like they've either been starved to death or recently escaped from prison.

I can't decide if I'm relieved or ready to fight them with a chair.

"Come in, come *in*." A sweet, motherly voice pops out of the silence behind us. We turn, seeing an older woman wearing a waitress uniform. "You must be freezing to death! Come on over here by the fire."

I don't hesitate. It's a huge fire, throwing off an amazing amount of heat. I sit on the edge of the mantle and hold my hands out, loving the pure warmth it emanates.

"Where did you come from?" the woman asks, tossing a wet towel over her shoulder. Just like a waitress. "What's your story?"

I swallow, exchanging a look with Chris. His face is expressionless as he shrugs off his jacket, revealing a long sleeved wool shirt.

"We're from the city," Chris replies.

He doesn't offer any more information. Wise.

"What is this place?" I ask, turning questions around.

"It *was* my business," she replies, sighing. "But ever since everything happened...well, I've just been using it as long as I can to help out people traveling through here. There's nothing else in these hills, and I can't get down the mountain very well during the dead of winter. Besides, with the stories I've been hearing, it's safer up here anyway."

I nod.

"That's for sure."

She raises an eyebrow.

"If you're from the city, what are you doing up here?" she asks.

"We're looking for my brother," Chris says. Such an easy lie. "He was camping up here when the pulse hit."

"I'm sorry," she says, softening. "But the chances of finding him are slim, honey."

"I know." Chris suddenly turns his attention away from her and starts unbuttoning my jacket. He helps me out of it, pulling my gloves off. My fingers are red, maybe frostbitten.

"Let me get you some food and drinks," the woman says. "And by the way, my name's Tasha."

I smile.

"Thank you, Tasha."

Neither Chris nor I offer up *our* names. Now that we're on Omega's radar, it'd probably be better to keep that little nugget of information to ourselves.

"Can you feel your fingers?" Chris asks, firelight casting shadows across his face.

"They haven't fallen off yet, if that's what you mean," I smirk. "They're a little numb, yeah."

He frowns, clasping my hands together. He rubs them between his own hands. The friction helps restore my sense of touch.

"I don't trust her," Chris says quietly. "She's fishing."

"We just walked into her restaurant," I reply. "She's naturally going to be curious."

"No. Something's off," he insists. "Don't tell her anything she doesn't need to know. Agreed?"

I give him a mock Boy Scout salute.

"You have my word, captain."

Tash comes back with food. She gives us a plate of steaming meat and soup, along with some hot tea. When I ask Chris what kind of meat it is, he tells me that I don't want to know, so I shouldn't ask. It's tough, with a strange flavor that I've never tasted in meat before. Maybe it's venison…or bear meat.

Thankfully, I don't have this revelation until after I've eaten.

Chris and I scoot against the wall, close enough to the fire to enjoy its heat. The people scattered around the restaurant are equally as silent and suspicious as we are, so they don't bother us.

"Make yourselves at home," Tasha says, cleaning up the trays.

"Thank you so much," I reply.

She smiles.

"I'm glad to do it."

She disappears to who-knows-where. I press my head against Chris's shoulder and he wraps his arm around me. "Warm at last?" he asks, smiling against my hair.

"Yeah," I reply. "But we'll have to get cold again tomorrow." "Remember what I told you about thinking warm thoughts?"

"I remember."

"You're not thinking warm thoughts."

I roll my eyes. "Fine, sorry. Fuzzy socks, bathrobes, electric blankets, soft boots. All that jazz. There. I feel warm."

"You only feel warm because I'm touching you," he says, flashing one of his devilish grins. "Wouldn't you agree?"

"No. I'd say that it's because we're sitting next to a *fireplace*."

"Goodnight," he whispers, kissing my forehead. "Think you can handle the heat all night?"

I slap his arm.

"Yeah. I think I can," I grumble. His cheerful laughter is the last thing I hear before I doze off.

Chapter Fourteen

It sucks to be shaken out of a deep sleep.

The fire is still burning. I'm slumped across Chris at an uncomfortable angle. I rub my stiff neck before I look around the room. What woke me up? I don't remember. I heard a sound, didn't I? Why else would I wake up? Maybe Chris was snoring.

No. He never snores. Even in his sleep he's freaking stealthy.

"...Yes, I'm sure. Positive," someone says.

Ah, voices. It was voices I heard. I close my eyes and concentrate on listening, mildly interested in the conversation. It sounds like Tasha. She's talking to men.

"They were here a few days ago, looking for them," Tasha says, her voice rough. "The reward was pretty big, the way they told it."

I lick my lips, fists clenching around Chris's shirt.

"Chris," I whisper, nudging his chin with my head. "Wake up."

He stirs, squeezing me tighter.

"*Chris!* I think we were just compromised."

He opens his eyes, blinking off the fuzziness of sleep.

"What?"

"Shh. Listen."

He peers at the ceiling, straining to hear what I'm hearing.

"...A man and a woman. They didn't give me their names, but they fit the descriptions. And the picture that was on *his* military ID is definitely that man with her."

Chris's expression changes slightly.

"Guess this was a bad idea after all," he whispers.

"What do we do?" I say, barely breathing the words.

"We get out of here."

As quietly as I can, I crawl forward and pull my jacket off the mantel. It's warm and dry. I button it up, putting on my gloves. Chris does the same.

"They're in the kitchen," he whispers. "We can get out the front door."

I nod, afraid to speak. Tasha's voice is joined by a couple more male voices. They're talking about us. There's no doubt about that. Thank *God* I woke up and heard them.

What if they'd slit our throats in our sleep?

Chris and I move toward the entrance, silent. The rest of the refugees are sleeping. I wrap my fingers around the doorknob, locking eyes with Chris. I hesitate before I turn the knob.

We get the door open, blistering cold air slamming into my face. Apparently the snowstorm has finally hit, judging by the slivers of ice slapping me in the face.

Sadly, the door is louder than I remember. It makes a piercing, screeching noise as we swing it open. I freeze, holding my breath, as if pretending I didn't hear anything will make it go away.

No dice.

Right on cue, Tasha rushes out of the kitchen. Her happy face is gone, replaced by an angry one. Several men come out of the kitchen behind her, and as soon as their eyes fall on us, we face each other.

"Hey," I say weakly. "Just checking the weather." I hold my hand over the threshold, immediately getting plastered with snow. "It's...snowing. A lot."

I force a smile.

"Kill them," Tasha says, deadpan. "It's dead or alive."

"Worst service ever," I reply. "No five-star rating from me."

Chris grabs my arm. We dash outside, Tasha's cronies hot on our heels. As soon as we hit the outdoors, I'm blinded by flurries of snow and ice swirling through the air. The wind is whipping, the snow is deeper than ever, and it's all I can do to hang onto Chris's hand for dear life.

I can't see anything but Chris seems to have some sense of direction. As Tasha's buddies run after us, I count four men in pursuit.

"Omega's put out a reward for us?" I gasp, running uphill. Through trees. We're plunging into the forest, in the middle of the night, in a blizzard. Not a smart idea, but it's either this or get killed. "How can we be that important to them?"

Chris's reply is lost in the storm as he drags me up the hill.

The men are gaining on us. I can't see them, but I can hear their heavy footsteps – and their voices. Their language is vile and obscene.

Blinded by darkness and flurries of ice, my boot catches on a protruding rock. I pitch forward slam to the ground. Cold snow soaks through my gloves.

"Cassidy, get up," Chris breathes, turning to help me.

"Look out!" I warn.

One of the thugs rams into his side, sending them both down the hill in a tumble of arms and legs. I struggle to my feet, losing them in the dark.

Another man appears from behind a tree, little more than a shadow. I take a step back. Why didn't I have the common sense to grab some kind of a weapon before we bolted out of the restaurant?

Wait.

I stick my hand under my jacket, feeling for my belt. Yes! The knife that Jeff gave me is snug against my skin, sheathed in a leather case. I pull it out, holding it in front of me to keep him away.

"I'll kill you," I warn. Lie. "Back off."

The shadow man laughs.

"I'm going to kill you either way," he says. "You're worth a lot of money."

He lunges. I take a few steps backward and dance away from him. He swipes at me again, and I twist my body to stay out of his reach. In broad daylight that wouldn't be possible, but in the dark storm it's not hard for him to miscalculate distance.

My luck can't hold out forever, though. I end up diving to the ground when he gets too close, scrambling away. He grabs my leg and drags me back. I kick upwards, hoping my foot connects with something.

It doesn't.

Fighting in real life is nothing like the movies, I think absently.

He pins me to the ground, hovering over me. He's close enough for me to see his dirty face.

I kick and bite and squirm under his weight but it's no good. He weighs a lot more than I do. He's not going anywhere.

He's going to kill me.

At that moment I feel him shift the position of his left arm, which means he's no longer pinning down *mine*. He's gripping something. A knife?

Jeff's knife is still in my hand, but it's turned away from my body, stuck underneath my leg. I thrust forward with my knees enough to relieve the pressure from his weight. Long enough for me to move the knife up and jam it as hard as I can into his arm.

He screams. I do, too. I kick him off, never loosening my grip on Jeff's knife, and sprint. Something wet and warm slicks over my hand. Blood. His or mine? I don't know.

"Chris?!" I yell, the wind whipping my hair around my face. "Chris!"

I can't see anything, hear anything, or feel anything except the cold. I bump into a tree and dig my fingers into the bark, a desperate attempt to orient myself.

"Chris," I breathe.

I sink to the ground and huddle against the tree, shielding myself from the snow cutting into my exposed skin. I keep low to the ground, stay still and listen. There's definitely background noise going on – voices, lots of yelling. I know Chris is close, but I can't *see* him. The frustration is palpable.

Crunch, crunch.

Footsteps. I tense.

Closer. Closer.

There's a bush a few feet away from me. It shakes. *Crack.* There goes a branch. More footsteps. My killer has returned. He's clutching his knife, breathing hard. Swearing. Holding his wounded arm.

Wrapped in a dark coat and hat, I remain motionless on the ground, holding my breath. He can't see me. I try not to breathe. The seconds tick by. An eternity.

He takes a few steps toward me, moving with all the grace of an elephant. I slide backwards, crawling beneath the undergrowth.

Be one with the shrub.

Minutes pass. My muscles are screaming, rebelling against my abnormal stillness. I ignore them and keep covered. I have no idea how much time passes before I hear footsteps again, more cautious than the previous pair.

I pray to God that whoever it is won't walk into me. That would destroy my whole *don't get killed* strategy. The footsteps get closer, but from which direction? I can't tell. The wind is too powerful, distorting the noise. Ice cuts across the surface of my eyes, burning my vision.

Snow is torture.

"Cassidy...?"

His voice is a faint whisper, but I hear it. I scramble to my feet, knocking branches and snow out of my way as I stumble around in the dark. "Chris! Where are you?"

"Here. Shhh. Don't yell." Chris's voice is much closer. I whirl around, smacking into his chest.

"Ouch!" I hold my nose between my hands. "That was unnecessarily painful."

"Take my hand," Chris says, feeling for my arm. "Are you hurt?"

"No. How long have I been hiding in the shrub?"

"You hid under a shrub?" An unusually powerful gust of wind howls through the trees. "Never mind. Just follow me."

I decide to take no chances on losing him again. I stick my hand through his belt, getting a firm grip.

We hike uphill for a substantial distance before I finally yell,

"Where are we going? We're lost, aren't we?"

"No!"

"Chris, we're going to freeze to death!"

We practically have to scream at each other to be heard.

"You know this area!" Chris finally shouts. "If you have any ideas, I'm game!"

"I don't know *everything* about this area! We just need to find shelter!"

I notice that Chris is bent over. I kneel next to him and put my head close to his face so he can hear me.

"What's wrong?" I ask. "Are you hurt?"

"Just got nicked," he replies, his voice breaking off.

Oh, great. He's hurt. Now what?

I slide his arm over my shoulders. He's not limping, but he seems disoriented. Absent, almost.

"Trust me," I say, trying to keep his spirits up. And mine. "I got this."

Chris's breath is warm on my cheek – and that's the only warmth I've got. If we don't find shelter soon, we'll both freeze to death. A morbid and unflattering way to die.

No. I won't die like that.

I slough through the snow.

Warm thoughts, right? If I think warm, I will become warm.

Eventually I drop to my knees, bringing Chris down with me. His breathing is labored, and I can feel his body tighten under my hands.

"Where are you hurt?" I ask.

"Chest, I think. Got...stabbed."

He's been *stabbed*? God, what am I supposed to do? What's going to happen to us?

Don't be afraid, I think. *Chris is always the one who takes control of the situation. Now it's your turn. Do the right thing.*

I force myself to keep going.

We keep walking until I find a rock. A huge rock; a boulder. I hunker behind it, realizing something important:

It's blocking the wind.

I drop, trembling excessively, and zip open my backpack. I find my flashlight and flick it on. It's barely enough illumination for what I need. I pull my gloves taut, and I dig until I have a trench about five feet wide and seven feet long. I grope blindly in the darkness for broken pieces of undergrowth, like small branches and pine needles. I lay them in the bottom of the trench for insulation.

Thirty minutes. Chris is still breathing hard.

I pull out our portable blankets, along with plastic packets of hand warmers. I tear them out of the packaging and shove them down my shirt and Chris's.

I shine the flashlight over his coat, but I don't see any wound. I can't move my fingers enough to unbutton his coat, so I just roll it up. There is a bloody gash on the upper area of his chest. I probe the wound. It's not deep. Nothing severe. I check his eyes.

His pupils are dilated, glassy.

What he's really suffering from is a concussion. That's what must be causing the disorientation and confusion. He must have been beaten over the head.

"Chris...come on," I pant, easing him into the trench. He lies down on his back and I curl up beside him. He slips his arm underneath me and holds me close.

"You know more about survival than you let on," he breathes.

I spread the blankets over our bodies, snuggling into the miniature snow trench I've created. That, combined with the block of the boulder, keeps the biting wind from killing us.

We should conserve enough heat to make it through the night.

I hope.

Freezing to death was never on my list of top ten ways to die. No, my number one way to die was being wrapped in an electric blanket with Food Network on in the background.

This is *so* not as comforting.

The good news is, it's morning. I can see the trees and the snow. I can still feel my limbs, and Chris seems to be recovering. The snow is falling softly now. The wind let off during the night, and now I'm lying on my side, propped up on one arm.

Chris is smiling at me, which means he's *got* to be feeling better. And while it may not be anywhere near sunbathing temperature, I don't feel as cold as I did last night.

"You scared me," I say, raising an eyebrow. "I thought you were dying."

"I probably was." He grins. "But you knew that."

"Shut up."

He lifts himself up, wincing. Other than that, he looks good.

"You perform well under pressure," he remarks. "The trench was smart." He pauses. "I'm sorry I couldn't help."

"You got your bell rung," I say dryly, echoing my dad.

"I got beat over the head."

"I'm sorry." I kiss the top of his hair. "Are you okay now?"

"Much better."

I take a good look around.

"I know where we are," I say, shocked. "My dad and I hiked here from our cabin last year."

I stand up, stiff, and Chris follows my lead. There's no logical reason for me to recognize one grove of trees from another, but I know this place. Because the big rock that saved our lives is the same one I took my picture on last year.

"It's Lizard Rock," I state.

"*Lizard* Rock?" Chris repeats, incredulous.

"During the summertime, it's crawling with lizards," I reply.

I climb the side of the rock, careful not to slip on the ice.

"I'm king of the rock," I exclaim, playful. "And I know how to find the cabin from here. Follow me, please."

Chris doesn't look as amused as I am, but he follows me anyway. We walk through freshly fallen snow, avoiding leaving footprints when possible. The new snow will cover the tracks eventually, but if there's anybody still actively hunting for us, it's better to play it safe.

We make a long trek uphill. Chris still seems...*off*. But he's far better than last night.

"What did they do to you?" I ask. "Was it more than one guy?"

"Three guys," he replies.

"How'd you get out of that alive?"

He shrugs.

"I guess I shouldn't have asked," I tease. "A Navy SEAL never reveals his secrets. Sorry, Frogman."

He laughs. "Apology accepted. And how many did you battle?"

"Well, we can't all bring down seven in one blow, oh mighty tailor," I quip. "But I got away from one of them. Jeff's knife saved my life."

Chris stops walking.

He says softly, "You've changed."

"What are you talking about?"

He doesn't answer.

"How much longer, Cassidy?" he asks.

"We'll be there by night-time," I reply. "We must have walked miles in the storm. We're a lot closer to it than we were at Tasha's restaurant."

"I think that place is a front," he muses. "Refugees trying to get away from Omega camps and the military executions are going to run to the mountains. She's using it as a way to turn people in to Omega and rake in the reward money – and keep herself in their good graces."

"That's sick," I say, disgusted. "I can't believe this is real."

"But it is."

Obviously. Or I wouldn't be here.

I ask a question that's been eating at me for the last few days.

"How many people do you think planned this takeover?" I say. "It's *got* to be more than just California. I'll bet all of the other states got hit with the EMP, then people panicked, Omega rolled in and everything just fell into place. It's genius."

"It is." He shakes his head. "All we can do now is fight."

"You mean literally or metaphorically speaking?"

"Both."

He doesn't elaborate. I'm not sure what he means.

Or perhaps I *do*. And that's slightly scary.

"Chris?"

He kneels beside me, tracing his finger along the snow.

"A footprint," he says. "Look."

He points to one. Then several more. My chest seizes up.

"Omega?" I whisper.

"I don't know. These are fresh. Not more than an hour."

I close my eyes.

Really? Again?

"Keep going," Chris tells me, squeezing my shoulder. "It's going to get dark and there's no reason for us to stop walking."

I shudder – but it's definitely not from the cold.

It's already late afternoon.

"We're here," I breathe, my anticipation heightening.

Dad. He's right over this hill.

We climb a small knoll lined with thick Manzanita bushes. It's dark and shadowed here, surrounded by redwoods, firs, cedars and pines. Nestled within the forest is a cabin made of clapboard wood. There's no road leading to it – just a trail that disappears every year with each storm.

It's our cabin.

I whoop with joy, tears coming to my eyes.

"We made it!!" I say, throwing my arms around Chris's waist.

"Cassidy, *think*," he replies, grabbing my shoulders. "There are footprints *everywhere*. We might not be alone."

I slowly comprehend his words. Right. The possibility of danger is still real. Very real.

Back to being cautious.

Chris warns me to stay behind his shoulder. He pulls his rifle out. Loaded. Ready.

"You're not going to use that, are you?" I ask. "*That* will be loud."

He ignores my remark.

We approach the cabin at an angle, staying away from the windows. The area around the cabin is coated in thick snow, and although they're faint, the remnants of footprints are everywhere.

They've got to be Dad's. There's no other explanation.

Chris edges up against the cabin edge, silent. Stealthy. We listen for sounds inside the cabin. Hearing nothing, we drop to our stomachs and crawl underneath the front windows.

Still, silence.

My heart is beating in my throat. Chris draws himself up to his full height, casting a glance at me. He shrugs, as if to say, "What have we got to lose?" and kicks in the door.

It crashes and shudders...because it's not locked. I spring up, panic tearing through me.

No, no, no, no, no.

I shove in front of Chris and run inside. It's got one room with an open loft above the kitchen. There's a table, a fireplace and a pile of bedding stacked against the wall.

But it's empty.

I spin in a circle, turning to Chris. He's not looking at me, though. He's looking at the back of the door, which he's shut behind us.

There's a white piece of paper nailed to it – a warrant straight out of Robin Hood.

I tear it off, hands shaking.

Oh, my God...

Under Penalty of LAW:

A Warrant of Arrest for

FRANK HART

For storing and hoarding supplies rightfully allotted to emergency services, possessing dangerous weapons, and failing to enroll in Omega's urgent CENSUS.

This property is hereby confiscated by the

FEDERAL GOVERNMENT

For use in emergency relocation programming and redistricting.

FURTHER

A WARRANT OF ARREST for

CASSIDY ELEANOR HART

And

CHRISTOPHER YOUNG

Co-conspirators wanted for treason and attempted murder.

"They expected to find us here with him," I gasp. "My God, Chris. They took him. They arrested him. They *killed* him."

I grip the paper, appalled.

No. This is exactly what I prayed wouldn't happen.

"You don't know that he's dead," Chris replies, grabbing me. He holds me there, refusing to allow me to move. "Look around you. There's no sign of a struggle. He might not even *be* here yet."

I gaze through him. Out of it.

I see Dad's backpack on the floor.

"No…" I whisper.

I break free of Chris's arms and kneel on the ground. It's a standard-issue pack, and I can see that most of the supplies are gone. My dad's name is stitched on the side of it. I know, because I'm the one who talked him into getting the backpack personalized a few years ago.

Its contents have been spilled across the floor, and when I follow the line of debris from the backpack into the kitchen, I see a broken bowl on the tile.

"He was here," I state, horrified. "They *did* take him. He's as good as dead."

I cover my mouth with my hands, biting a silent scream.

"You don't know that he's dead," Chris repeats, but he doesn't sound too sure. "Cassie…?"

I don't answer him, because I can't. I'm too busy crying.

Dad's gone.

Chapter Fifteen

When I was eight-years-old, I watched a scary movie that my parents had specifically told me *not* to. I'd seen the DVD lying around the house and I thought I'd turn it on, and once I did, I couldn't turn it off.

I had the worst nightmares of my life that night.

Dad, instead of punishing me for watching the movie, brought me a nightlight and plugged it into the electric socket in my room. He told me it would keep the scary thoughts away. As long as the light was on, I was safe.

I kept that nightlight until the EMP hit. And now, all I can think about is the irony of that belief. We're not safe. We never were. Society was an illusion. A mask. Beneath it, all hell was waiting to break loose.

And not even my dad could survive it.

I press my face against Chris's shoulder.

"We'll find him," Chris says, over and over. "I promise."

Thank God for Chris. I don't deserve him.

"What now?" I whisper, hoarse.

"We sleep."

"I can't sleep."

"Yes, you can. You're exhausted. We both are."

"I just lost everything." I sniff. "What's the point of sleeping or eating or *caring*? They're just going to keep taking things away from us until they kill us. First our cars, our cellphones, our houses. Then our lives. They're not going to stop. They'll take everything."

"You're wrong, Cassidy," Chris replies, his voice even. "They haven't taken everything from you *or* me. They haven't taken *us*. Who we are. They can't take our souls. They can try to kill us and subjugate us, but I sure as hell won't go down without a fight."

I take a shaky, painful breath.

"Why fight?" I ask. "They'll kill us. Just like they killed all those people at the rest stop and in Bakersfield. Just like they killed Bree. We're outnumbered, outgunned, and out-strategized. We're screwed and you know it."

"We're alive," Chris answers, taking my face between his hands. "We're together. We're a team, and they can't change that."

I suck in my breath.

"We're a team?" I echo, tired. "Are you sure about that?"

Chris chuckles. It's an exhausted but sincere sound.

"I'm sure," he says, kissing my forehead. "And I'm here for you, no matter what happens. We're in this together."

I wrap my arms around his neck, tears running down my face.

"We're a team," I tell him, and I mean it. "I trust you."

It's true. I *do* trust him. I can't think of anyone who could protect me like he does. At any rate, maybe I'll feel differently about things in the morning. Maybe I'll feel more optimistic. Maybe my dad *is* alive.

But finding him...how is *that* supposed to happen?

First rule of the new world: don't hoard. All of the supplies that my dad and I brought to this cabin have been taken by Omega. Everything. Every drop of water, every flake of dehydrated chicken breast. All we've got is what Chris's mom gave us, and even then it's a miracle we have anything left.

232

Apparently, nobody but the big dogs are allowed to have supplies. Makes a lot of sense if you're trying to subjugate people. What better way to control the populace than to control the food supply? People will do anything when they're starving.

It's about eight o'clock at night. We've draped heavy blankets over the windows and stuffed rags in the cracks around the doors. Only then do we light a couple of lanterns. I'm curled up on the loft bed above the kitchen, watching Chris get some food together. He's making coffee with our camping stove and heating up leftover biscuits.

"I'll cook," I volunteer, sliding down the ladder.

"Rest, Cassie," he advises, without turning around. "You're tired."

"I don't want to rest. And I happen to be a biscuit expert." I sit on the edge of the makeshift counter. "Coffee at night? Really?"

"As soon as the storm settles down we need to get back home," he replies, placing one hand on each side of me. "Are you up for that?"

No. Just the thought of doing *anything* right now is sickening.

"Sure," I lie. "Sounds good."

He raises his eyebrows, obviously not buying it.

"Coffee's burning," I say.

He turns around, snatching it off the stove before it scorches.

There are still some dishes left in the cupboard. Stuff from thrift stores that my dad and I bought cheaply to bring up here. What good did it do? Without food or water...or *Dad*...things are pointless.

"Have you checked that knife wound?" I ask as he pours the coffee.

He hands me a cup.

"No," he replies. "I was getting around to it."

"Better hurry up. The last thing we need is for you to get an infection and die," I say, trying to smile.

Chris brushes my cheek with the back of his hand. "You're right."

He walks to the other side of the cabin – which is only about twenty feet in length – and digs through his backpack. I take a sip of the coffee, almost spitting it out. "It's bitter."

"Coffee generally is," Chris laughs, rolling the first aid kit out on the counter. "It'll make you feel better."

"Why? Trying to turn me into a caffeine addict?"

"That's the plan." Chris pulls off his jacket, revealing the bloodstain on his wool shirt. It's not as bad as I thought. "What do you think?"

"I think I'm not the addiction type."

He runs a hand over his mouth, hiding a smile.

"I was talking about the blood, Cassie."

"Oh. Looks okay."

He rolls up the shirt enough to get a good view of the cut. It's not very deep, but nicked enough to get infected if left untreated. Chris looks at me.

"Can you stitch it?" he asks.

I swallow a lump in my throat – I've never been good with first-aid stitching – and nod. "Sure," I say. "I need the antiseptic wipes."

He dumps the first aid kit on the counter and opens his arms out wide.

"Be my guest."

I find the wipes, the needle, the thread. If you even *call* it thread. I stifle a shudder and flip open the emergency handbook. There are directions for stitching up a wound. I've practiced in the past on a dummy – a routine my dad periodically had me do because, "You just never know when you might need the skill."

Thanks for the tip, *Dad*.

I follow the instructions step by step, holding back a gag as I clean the wound and touch the disconnected piece of skin. So. Nasty.

"Fun times," I complain.

Chris just grunts.

Weaving in and out of the flesh with the needle is enough to make me puke, but I fight the urge. I feel pleased with myself when I'm done. I close the stiches like the book says and set down the needle.

"There. You're a regular ragdoll now."

Chris inspects my handiwork. It's a little uneven, but hey. At least I did it.

"Not bad," he comments. "Thanks."

He lets his shirt drop and I clean the needle with an antiseptic wipe.

"Does it hurt?" I ask, putting everything back in the kit.

"Nah. You?"

"I didn't get wounded," I remind him.

"You know what I mean."

I shut my mouth, not because I'm speechless, but because if I start to talk, I may cry. And I don't want to cry. I can't.

"Cassie, we'll find him," Chris says, touching my arm. "We got this far, didn't we?"

"Yeah, and he wasn't here." I turn around.

Are my eyes as red as I think they are?

"Who knows where they took him, Chris? It could be anywhere." I run a hand through my hair and toss the first-aid kit across the room. "He's gone. There's nothing we can do."

"There's always something."

Chris takes my hand, pressing it against his chest. He's warm, and I can feel his heart beating in a steady rhythm under his skin.

"As long as we're both alive," he says, tipping my chin up, "and our hearts are still beating, there's still a chance. I won't go down without a fight, and I know you won't either. *That* gives us a chance, Cassie."

I meet his firm gaze, and what I see there is encouraging. Exhaustion? Yes. A little uncertainty? You bet. But there's also hope, and if Chris is still holding onto it, maybe it's not so bad after all.

I hug him tightly. Chris folds me into his arms and kisses the top of my head. "Listen to me," he says. "Do you remember when we saw the dead bodies at the camp in Bakersfield?"

"Yes," I nod.

"Those were systematic executions. There was no real reason for those. They do that to scare people into submission. People like you and me? They'll make an example out of us. Just to scare the crap out of people. Labeling us as war criminals is perfect for frightening the populace into submission. People like you and me and your dad. Why would they bother with an arrest warrant for the three of us when Omega is killing whoever they want? Think about it. Three people out of millions? Why would they care where we go?"

I pull away and look into his face.

Light bulb.

"Because they need to keep the population under control," I say, swallowing. "And killing off the few survivors or resistors will scare people from getting any ideas about rebelling."

He leans closer, and I can smell the coffee on his breath.

"Exactly." He brushes the hair out of my eyes. "And it's a fact that they don't usually execute those "examples" right away. They drag it out. They take them somewhere."

My eyes widen.

"They take them to prison."

"Someplace where they can publicize the whole thing."

"But where?"

Chris smiles.

"I guess we'll just have to find out, won't we?"

I groan. "Are you kidding me? We just *got* here!"

But there is no real annoyance in my voice. I trust Chris.

He places his hands on each side of my waist.

"You'll survive," he says. "You always do."

I grit my teeth. Even if there were any chance of locating my dad again, it would mean that we'd have to trek across the former heartland of California on foot through hostile territory. Again.

"We'll wait until the storm dies down," Chris tells me, as if reading my thoughts. "Then we'll head back toward my house, check in with my parents, and try to figure this thing out. We'll come up with a plan."

"Yeah," I say. "We always do."

Chapter Sixteen

I've always loved hiking.

Today, I hate it. I've been walking endlessly for weeks now, and I don't think it's ever going to end.

It took us a week to get back to Squaw Valley because of the heavy storms, slushy terrain, crappy food supply and possible detection by people trying to sell us out to Omega hacks. Now we're less than a half a mile away from the Young property, and I can tell by the look on Chris' face that he's happier than I am to be home.

And that's saying something.

It's not snowing at this elevation, which is fine with me. My fascination with snow has officially ended, and I can easily live without it. The trees here are spindly, what my dad would call "sky roots."

Poor Dad.

Nope, don't go there, I think. *Stay focused.*

"I'm going to have a whole fried chicken when we get there," I say, grinning at Chris. "What about you?"

"My dad's got a stash of beer in the basement," he replies. "I could use a case or two."

"Great. Fried chicken and beer. All we need is a pickup and a parking lot and we could be a couple of football fans," I say. "You *do* watch football, right?"

"Baby, I *played* football," Chris replies, picking up the pace.

"You went to high school?" I say, puzzled. "I thought you went through a charter school like Jeff."

"No," he shakes his head. "I went all the way through. And I was the star quarterback." He winks.

I roll my eyes.

"How modest."

"I took the *Lions* to the championships."

"Why am I not surprised?"

"You would have been a cute cheerleader," he comments.

"Are you *kidding*?"

We laugh. He makes a move to grab me around the waist but I run forward, fueled by a surge of excitement to reach his home. I jog a bit, rounding the next corner. My footsteps come to an abrupt stop when my gaze lands on a group of trees and bushes on the side of the road. It's not the shrubbery that draws my attention. It's the *lack* of it. Charred, black, sooty ashes line the ground.

Everything is burned.

Chris' steady footsteps come up behind me. His face is a hard mask that betrays no emotion. He swings his gun into his hands and releases the safety switch.

"Stay behind me," he says, his voice dangerous.

"But..."

He gives me a look that says, "Don't argue."

I don't.

I stay behind his shoulder as we approach the wall of trees and bushes that once hid the nearly invisible dirt trail that led to the Young property. The grass is gone. The weeds are burned. Even the trees are dead.

A lead weight settles in my stomach.

We walk faster up the dirt trail. Fear and adrenaline rush through me – through *both* of us. Tire tracks are everywhere, nearly washed away in the mud.

It takes us about ten minutes to reach the top of the hill.

Chris swears.

I drop to my knees, not wanting to see what I'm seeing.

The house has been burned to the ground.

And the Young family is nowhere in sight.

Epilogue

It's a funny thing. The world, I mean.

When the EMP hit, I kept thinking that it was the end of the world...but is it really? Didn't people live without cars and phones and electricity for thousands of years? The only thing that makes this different from the seventeenth century is the fact that few people know how to live without technology. Even fewer know how to accept the fact that there are very real bad guys out there trying to take away the things that are most important to us.

Then again, maybe it's already happened in the past and we just didn't realize it until it happened to *us*. Because isn't that usually the case? People don't understand how something bad could happen until it happens to *them*.

And so here I am, my boots propped up on an old log with my head in Chris' lap. He's fiddling with my hair, but his eyes are focused on something in the distance. The gold chain he gave me is hanging around my neck, the metal cool against my collarbone as we sit silently in the woods. I find comfort in the touch of his fingers on my skin. It reminds me that I still have something, *someone*, to hold onto.

A burnt home, destroyed crops, slaughtered animals and a missing family?

Check that off the list of sucky things that have happened to us in the last two months. With nowhere to go and nothing to eat, what can we do but go ahead with our plan to find out where they're imprisoning the war criminals?

Chris needs to find his family. I need to find my dad.

We need each other, and for the record, that's the only thing right about this messed up new world: Us.

We'll find a way. Chris is smart. He knows how to survive in a world like this. I'm not as skilled as he is when it comes to survival, but I'm learning quickly. I *will* find my father. We *will* find the Young family and Isabel again. And if anybody gets in our way?

I guess I'll just have to shoot them.

Right between the eyes.

To Be Continued in
STATE OF CHAOS
Collapse Series #2

More Titles from WB Publishing:

Continue Cassidy Hart's story in:

State of Chaos: Collapse Series #2 by Summer Lane

State of Rebellion: Collapse Series #3: by Summer Lane

Coming June 6th, 2014: State of Pursuit: Collapse Series #4:
by Summer Lane

WB Publishing is a digital publishing company devoted to releasing only the most exciting and engaging adventure stories in the dystopian, post-apocalyptic and survivalist genres. Do you have a story that you think would be great for us? Submit your manuscript here!

http://writingbellepublishing.com/

Acknowledgements

When I was thirteen, I dreamed of writing a book that I could share with people all over the world. Thanks to Cassidy Hart, that dream has come true. *The Collapse Series* has been a miracle, an amazing blessing. I have no one but God to thank for that.

This revised edition of *State of Emergency* was a fun project to undertake – albeit a massive amount of work. *State of Emergency* was originally penned for the sheer fun of it, but it has become my most successful work to date. My parents were integral in encouraging me to release it to the world – and for that I will be forever grateful. The advice and guidance from James P. White was priceless, a gift I will always be thankful for. And of course, thanks to my brother. You're the best friend I'll ever have.

Thank you Ellen Mansoor Collier, for being a lovely friend and for helping make the revised edition of *State of Emergency* a reality. To my grandfather, Pete, for being the brightest light in my life. You taught me that there is no such word as "impossible." To my grandmother, Nancy, for always being my friend! Thank you to the writing community, bloggers and book reviewers who supported me when I was just starting out. The optimism and encouragement I received from *all of you* was and still is priceless.

When *State of Emergency* became a bestseller, I was pleasantly surprised and amazed. Cassidy Hart's story is one of a very average girl in a very extraordinary situation. I wrote it without inhibitions, with the intention of answering the question: what would happen if everyone were forced to survive without technology of any kind? No cars, no electricity, no indoor plumbing and no food from the grocery store. The conclusion I drew after finishing *State of Emergency* was rather depressing. I think our society is amazingly dependent on technology. I know *I* certainly am! How different our world is than twenty years ago – or even ten. It's an interesting thought. But in the end, I believe that there will always be people like Cassidy Hart and Chris Young. People who will take the initiative, do the right thing and survive.

Because survival is what it's all about. Right?

Last – but certainly not least – I want to thank my Lord and Savior, Jesus Christ. Storytelling is my passion, and because of you I can make a career out of what I love most!

Philippians 4:13

About the Author

Summer Lane is the author of the National Bestselling *Collapse Series,* which currently includes *State of Emergency*, *State of Chaos*, *State of Rebellion* and *State of Pursuit*. Summer owns *WB Publishing,* a digital publishing company devoted to releasing only the most exciting and engaging adventure stories. In her spare time, Summer is the creator of the online magazine, *Writing Belle*. She also works as a consultant, freelance writer and creative writing teacher.

Summer began writing when she was thirteen years old, due to the fact that the long afternoons after school were somewhat boring, and writing stories seemed to make the time pass a little quicker. Since then, she has written many stories about jungle cats, secret agents, princesses and spaceships. You can find her hopping around Twitter @SummerEllenLane. Want to send her an email? Contact her at: summerlane101@gmail.com

Connect with Summer Lane:

Official Website:

http://www.summerlaneauthor.com/

Online Magazine:

http://writingbelle.com/

GoodReads:

https://www.goodreads.com/author/show/5823376.Summer_L
ane

Or Twitter:

https://twitter.com/SummerEllenLane

And Facebook:

https://www.facebook.com/pages/State-of-Emergency-
Collapse-Series/178664608947815

Want to talk to the author? Send her an email with any
question – she'd love to hear from you! Contact her at:

summerlane101@gmail.com

Made in the USA
Charleston, SC
03 October 2014